Karly's Wolf

Penny Alley

Karly's Wolf

by

Penny Alley

A Red Hot Romance Erotic Novel

All rights reserved.
Copyright 2013 © by Penny Alley

This book may not be reproduced, in whole or part, by mimeograph or any other means, without permission of the author.
thetarantularanch@yahoo.com

This book is a work of fiction.
Any resemblance to actual persons, places, and events are purely coincidental.

Edited by:
Rose Lipscomb

Cover design by:
Sarah-Jane Lehoux
Phylicia Raine Lafantasie

Formatted by:
Phylicia Raine Lafantasie

Also by Penny Alley:

Demon Seduction
Golden Song
Incubus Moon

Coming Soon!

Gabe's Bride

PROLOGUE

Digging her keys from her jeans pocket, Karly shoved through the screen door hard enough to send it crashing back against the house. Her hastily-packed suitcase banged against her leg as she jogged down the steps and ran for her car. *Run, Run, RUN!*—it was the only thought in her head as she fumbled the keys into the lock. She looked back over her shoulder, already hearing Dan's heavy work boots pounding down the carpeted second-floor stairs in aggressive pursuit. Just as she yanked the car door open, he burst from the house after her.

"Get your ass back here!" His face was livid. His fists were tightly clenched. "Karly!" He leapt off the porch after her. "I'm not through with you!"

Yeah well, she was through with him. She was through with black eyes and cover-up that didn't cover enough, leaving people to stare at the marks his fits of temper often left behind. She was through alternating between being a punching bag and a doormat. She was just plain through.

Flinging her suitcase onto the passenger seat, Karly jumped behind the wheel, yanking her feet in and quickly slamming the door seconds before he hit the side of her car. She slapped the locks down just as he grabbed the handle and the whole car shook as he punched, kicked and shoved in frustration. He slammed his fist into the window, but the glass withstood the blow far better than his knuckles did. Twirling, a burly ballerina of pain in his policeman's uniform, Dan hugged his hand to his chest and spat curses into the lawn between his feet.

Shaking so badly that she almost dropped her keys, Karly started the car and his attention locked on her again.

"Where do you think you're going? Karly!" When the engine revved, Dan darted behind the car. He slammed both hands flat against the trunk, his dark eyes wild and promising more than just a black eye if she didn't start "paying attention." Love, honor and obey; that's what she'd promised and Dan, as he was fond of saying, refused to accept anything less.

So, you'd better start paying attention, little girl... She shuddered, her hands gripping white-knuckled at the wheel.

"Don't," Dan warned, soft and low, his gaze locked with hers in the rearview mirror. Icy fingers prickled up her spine. He was always at his most dangerous when his voice went soft and low. "Don't do anything stupid, baby. I'll make you regret it, I swear to God."

That was the wrong thing for him to say.

Half-scared and half-angry, Karly shoved the gears into reverse and stomped the gas pedal to the floor. He dove out of the way just in time. Otherwise, she'd have run him over and she wasn't at all sure if she'd feel bad about it afterward or not. As it was, she left twin streaks of black rubber lining the length of the driveway and then she was gone, peeling off down the quiet residential street without any regard for speed. Her only thought was to get away. Run. Escape. She had been planning it for months.

She gripped and re-gripped the steering wheel, checking the rearview just as Dan's bright red pickup barreled out of the garage in furious pursuit.

He was never going to let her go. Karly burst into tears. She didn't know she was going to until it just happened. She also stomped the gas pedal again, speeding straight through the stop sign on the corner. She was gasping, trying to pull herself back under control and praying none of Dan's cop buddies would be stationed at the well-known speed trap opposite the liquor store.

One was.

The black and white started to pull out behind her. She saw the minute flash of his lights and heard the brief blip of a siren's wail before the unknown policeman spotted Dan's truck. Both lights and sirens shut off. Small town cops stuck together, offering more blame than protection to the battered wife of one of their own.

She had to get out of Redemption. If she could make it to the highway, then she might have a chance. The state patrol was headquartered just two miles down the road. State cops were still cops, still part of that same "stick together no matter what" fraternity, but they were also less likely to overlook black eyes on hysterical wives. Sometimes, they even asked questions.

Karly kept going, driving as fast as her little Honda could, knuckling away the tears that kept leaking out and wincing each time she touched her right eye. It was swelling, red and getting redder by the second. She could already see spots of darkness growing up under the puffy skin, but at least she could still see out of it well enough to keep tabs on Dan in the rearview.

He was keeping pace with her, but not doing anything aggressive. She could see him behind the wheel, smoking a cigarette and muttering. Probably cussing her, or reassuring himself of all the things he was going to do once he got her home again—

His hand on the back of her neck...his belt whipping down again and again until she was screaming apologies into the bedspread...

She gripped the steering wheel, her palms starting to sweat. Well, his gas gauge was broken and she knew something he didn't. Two nights back, just like clockwork, Dan had filled his gas tank, but in the wee small hours this morning while he had slept, Karly had siphoned out as much as she could, putting ten gallons in her car and another five in the two storage cans in her trunk. If he wasn't driving on fumes just yet, he would be soon enough. All she had to do was watch, wait, and keep on driving.

Run, run, run!

She was past city hall, past the Wal-Mart at the last stop light and almost to the highway before Dan's truck gave its first sputtering hint of impending failure. It jerked, rapidly reducing in speed, and by the time he got it pulled over onto the gravel roadside, she could see him beating on the steering wheel with both fists.

"Who's paying attention now?" Karly said bitterly, and barely slowed at all as she took the on-ramp out of town. Once Redemption was out of sight, she let her speed drop back to something approaching normal. After that, she was safe, she knew. She didn't have to keep checking the rearview mirror. She didn't have to keep looking over her shoulder.

Some habits, however, are really hard to break.

CHAPTER ONE

    Hollow Hills was an old copper-mining town with a population sign that boasted 397 people. It sat in a geographical pocket, surrounded by mountains and national forests and flanked by Wallow Creek, which was in actuality more of a lake than a creek. But it was quiet and remote, with a thriving tourist trade during hunting and fishing seasons. It was also located two states away, and Dan would never think to look for her here. She could have blinked and driven right through town without even realizing it.
    There was no light and no stop signs, just a handful of old Wild-West-style buildings situated right off a winding two-lane highway. The general grocery store, gas station, feed store (which doubled as a post office) and breakfast diner (which closed every afternoon at two and never opened at all on Sundays) sat on the left-hand side of the road. The local station house for Fish and Game sat back off the highway on the right behind a thin curtain of trees, making it difficult to notice. And that was it, the sum total of consumer life in Hollow Hills. When Karly first called to inquire about a tiny cabin advertised for rent, Margo Hemington had told her most everybody who lived here had done so for generations, refusing to leave even after the copper mines shut down.
    "If you want to get away, you can't get much farther than Hollow Hills," Margo had proudly stated. "City folk don't usually stick around beyond what it takes them to fish or hunt. Cabin's got no phones. No internet or TV, and cellphones can get a bit sketchy on whether they'll work or not. It's got electric though. I put that in a couple years back. Even has proper plumbing. No outhouse."
    "Sounds perfect," Karly had said. "If I pay six months in advance, will you keep the utilities in your name?"
    The pause that had followed had only lasted half a heartbeat.

"I can do that," Margo finally said, and the deal had been struck.

As soon as Karly pulled into town, she called Margo to arrange a meeting at Emmett's Hay and Feed to exchange money for the keys and directions to the cabin. While she waited, Karly opened her suitcase and dug out the small coffee can where she'd hidden every cent she could pilfer out of her paychecks and the weekly allotment Dan had allowed for groceries. All of that amounted to little more than four hundred dollars. The rest—thirty-six thousand and change—had come from her mother just days before she'd died.

"I buried it under the front porch steps," Ezie Barker had rasped from her hospital bed. "Go and dig it up. Then you take it, baby girl, and you run."

No mention of that money made it into the reading of Ezie's will, which was just as well. Karly had been her mother's only child and sole heir, but everything that had been left to her, Dan had taken.

Counting out six months' worth of utilities and rent, Karly slipped the wad, plus a little extra, in her pocket. Hiding the can in the bottom of her suitcase again, she went into the general store. She bought a few cleaning supplies, a toothbrush (because in her haste to get out, she'd forgotten hers) and something quick and easy to fix for dinner: a small package of ground beef and generic-brand hamburger helper. By the time she emerged from the store, the shadows cast by the surrounding evergreens were long, the sun was going down, and an old woman dressed in worn jeans and a flannel shirt was waiting for her on the feed store steps.

Stashing her supplies in the car, Karly made her way across the parking lot. "Ms. Hemington?"

"Margo," the old woman replied, gruff and business-like. She stood up, brushing the dust off the seat of her jeans and stuck out her work-rough hand. She looked at Karly and then pointedly at Karly's black eye. Though she'd tried to smooth her too-long bangs down far enough to hide that side of her face, the bruise extended too far down her cheek. There was no pretending it didn't exist. "Well," she said. "You're well shut of him, aren't you?"

The only thing worse than the bruise was the humiliation of someone else knowing exactly how she'd gotten it. Karly's knee-jerk instinct was to deny she'd been hit. A good fall, feigned clumsiness, it was so much easier to admit to, except that Karly never got the chance.

Already the old woman was pulling out a set of keys and written directions, pressing both into Karly's hands as she said, "Go straight on out of town and take Old Bueller Road. It ain't marked, but it's your first unpaved on the right. Follow that on about four miles and past the dogwoods. McQueens live out there now, but don't you worry none. They aren't as like to shoot you for a stranger if you've got the keys. If they do go for their guns, you just tell their ma I sent you and she'll whoop that mangy lot straight!"

"O-okay." Karly stared at the directions and then at Margo. "Thanks."

The old woman patted her hand. "You're in a good place, girl. Around here, we know the good ones from the bad. Anyone coming to Hollow Hills looking for trouble will be lucky if trouble doesn't find them first! Go on. You've daylight enough to find the place if you hurry."

The paper of directions crinkled between Karly's hands as she looked at them and then back at Margo. The old woman couldn't possibly understand, but she hadn't just given Karly keys to some remote old cabin, she'd given her keys to a brand new start in life.

"Thank you," she tried to say again, but had to stop, afraid she might start crying. She didn't want to cry in front of Margo. That was the only thing more humiliating than being caught wearing fresh bruises.

"Go on," Margo said, waving her off with both hands. "Daylight's burning."

Karly returned to her car and lay her new house keys on the passenger seat. As she drove away, Margo offered a farewell wave and called, "Drive safe and mind the animals!"

Karly drove slowly, holding the directions against the steering wheel so she could keep a close eye on them. She found Old Bueller Road easily enough, but when she turned onto it, she found herself driving into the setting sun. Lush evergreens and sprawling oaks shielded her from the worst of the glare, but that blanket of road dust on her windshield turned every flash of sunlight she drove through into a blinding sheen of yellow and white. She held up a blocking hand, but still could barely see the road ahead.

Gravel, kicked up by the tires, peppered the underside of her car. She bounced from rut to runnel and over exposed tree roots, one of which was so large it scraped her oil-pan. Four miles became closer to five, and the 'dogwoods' were in actuality a weathered sign that read, 'Dog Woods'. It also had more bullet holes in it than letters and she began to get nervous, worrying at the edges of her paper as she strained to see through the blinding light and thickly-wooded overgrowth for signs of the McQueens.

Hers was an overactive imagination determined to conjure up deadly, dangerous hillbillies, hell-bent on protecting hidden moonshine stills or, worse, marijuana farms. She saw dozens of broken cars—rusted out vehicle shells that the forest and blackberry brambles struggled to hide, and by the time she glimpsed two narrow brown shacks, peeking back at her out from behind the cover of shadow and trees, Karly had truly spooked herself. A distant figure on the farthest porch stood up. Figuring her day had been rough enough without the added strain of being shot at, Karly sped up. She kept one eye on the half-hidden shacks and moved past them as quickly as possible, taking the sharp corner ahead much faster than she should have.

Sunlight pierced straight into her eyes and she threw up her hand again, striving to block the worst of it and barely spotting something dark directly in front of her just before it dashed to get out of the way. She stomped the brakes with both feet. Her car spun, fishtailing wildly and spraying dirt and rocks back into the trees. And still she felt that dreadful *whump* as whatever it was bounced off her front bumper and crashed into overgrown brush that lined the road.

"Oh my God." Kylie sat frozen behind the wheel, her heart pounding and her mouth agape, terrified that she'd just hit a man. "Oh my God!" Throwing the car into park, she fumbled to get the door open and her seatbelt off. She stumbled out of the car, finding no sign of whatever she'd hit in the bushes at first, but then she checked the bumper. Blood, that was the first thing she saw. Blood and a bushy tuft of long dark hair.

One hand clapped over her mouth and the other clutching her suddenly queasy stomach, Karly turned to stare into the shadowed bushes. At first hasty glance, she saw no hint that anything had recently disturbed this stretch of road. It wasn't until she crept closer and really looked that she saw broken twigs here, and crushed grass there, and then…something dark, lying in the blackest part of the shadows, silent and unmoving.

Creeping closer, Karly bent to peer into the brush. It took her eyes a moment to recognize the thing lying there as a dog. A really big dog—like a Husky, maybe. She didn't know much about dogs, but she'd seen those in a movie before, only this one was black all over, with thicker fur and sharper features. The horror that gripped her gut barely eased. Mind the animals, Margo had said, and here she'd gone and killed someone's dog.

Karly inched closer still, squatting down a little in an attempt to get a better look. No, not killed. It was still breathing.

"Shh, it's okay," she whispered as she reached into the prickly bushes and touched its soft, dark flank. The fur felt wet and her fingers came away sticky with blood. "Oh baby, I'm so sorry!"

A broken whine was the only response. Wobbly and dazed, the dog raised its head. It tried to rise, but couldn't and flopped back down to lie there instead.

Was it the McQueens' dog? Karly stood up, stabbing her fingers through her long blonde hair as she stared back down the road toward the rundown shacks. Was she brave enough to walk back there and tell the gun-toting hillbillies that Margo had expressly warned her about, that she'd just hit their family pet? Her heart thumped twice, almost stopping in her chest.

No. No, she definitely was not.

She looked at the dog, then at her car, and then back down the winding dirt road and quickly made up her mind. Digging her coat out of the trunk, she cleared as much room as she could on her backseat.

"It's okay," she soothed as she crawled into the bushes with the injured dog. She wrapped her coat around him. "Please, please don't bite me."

It made her nervous, getting her face this close to a wounded animal, but dazed as he was, the dog only turned his head to look at her. He nosed at her cheek, but didn't growl and made absolutely no aggressive motions. Not even when she wrapped her arms under and around him and tried to lift.

He was bigger than he looked and heavy—she grunted—much heavier than she would have thought. In the end, after several heaving attempts that failed to budge the unsteady animal and afraid she might hurt him more if she continued trying, she spread her coat out on the ground and gently rolled him onto it. Gripping her coat sleeves, she dragged him back out of the vegetation onto the road.

Rocky as the ground was, it couldn't have been comfortable for him. Grunting and straining with every tentative pull, Karly had only just drawn abreast of the rear passenger door when the dog seemed to gather wits enough to try standing again. She stopped pulling, for fear she'd accidentally sweep his unsteady feet out from under him.

"Easy, puppy," she soothed, offering support until he locked his legs, gaining some stability. He was still weaving though, still dazed. "It's okay, baby. Easy. Easy." She reached past him to open the back. "Okay, up. Get inside."

Head hanging low, he stared into the backseat, but made no move to comply. Gradually, Karly let go of him and sat back on her heels, watching without breathing, halfway hoping he might simply shake off his wounded lethargy and lope off into the woods without any further interference from her.

It was an incredibly selfish moment for her, and one that she was heartily ashamed of as the seconds bled out into minutes and it became painfully obvious that the poor dog was anything but fine. He wobbled, he swayed. He took a single, faltering step, his front legs completely out of sync with the back and, in the end, Karly went back to her original plan.

"It's okay," she soothed as she wrapped her arms around his thick chest. One paw at a time, one step at a time, she muscled the heavy canine into the back of her car. She all but lifted his hind legs up onto the seat when he seemed incapable. Massive, furry and bloody, he lay where she left him, overflowing her rear seat and whining softly when she tried to tuck his rear limbs in out of the way of the door.

"It's okay," Karly said stupidly one last time. Her hand trembled, but she gave his massive head an impromptu pat in the hopes there would be no hard feelings when this was all over.

As she withdrew, he lifted his nose to lick the back of her retreating hand. His tail thumped twice, a halfhearted wag that dropped it back off the seat. She carefully brushed it up to lie over his rear legs and softly closed the car door. Then she stood there, staring in at the dog, who stared fixedly back at her with lupine yellow eyes.

Now what?

Bending, she picked her coat up off the ground and looked at the blood smears. She turned in a full circle, looking up and down both ends of the gravel road. Should she go back to town? Surely there had to be a vet...somewhere. If not in Hollow Hills, then maybe the next town over, wherever that was. And what about the cabin? The sun was going down, and it was getting very dark, very fast. If she lost what little daylight she had left, how would she ever find her way to the cabin?

It was her second moment of supreme and shameful selfishness, but when Karly got back in the car, instead of taking the dog where he could get medical help, she continued on.

She half wondered and maybe even expected the dog might be dead by the time that long and winding road culminated in a cul-de-sac in front of the small rental that was her new home. By now, the sun was completely gone and all she could see was black shadows set against a dark gray and star-studded sky. Set well back in the trees, the cabin blended with the shadows. Two narrow stories tall, each level seemed no larger than was required to house a single room, and it was dark. Not one welcoming light could be seen anywhere, apart from her own headlights reflecting back at her off the two front windows.

Shifting into park, Karly stared at the cabin. She had never lived on her own before. She had left college and her mother's house for marriage with Dan—a four-year descent that had taken her from happy straight into hell. Now she was alone.

Well, but that wasn't true anymore, was it?

Glancing into the rearview mirror, she looked at the injured dog sprawled across the seat behind her. It was too dark to see him clearly, but she could hear his panting breaths, so she knew he was still alive.

She really should take him to a vet. That was the decent thing to do. But she didn't. She took the keys out of the ignition instead.

"I'll be right back," she told him, trying to swallow her guilt as she pushed open the driver's side door. The dog watched while she got out, following her with his eerie yellow eyes.

Engulfed in the glow of the headlights, Karly climbed the front porch steps and unlocked the front door. In many ways, the cabin was better on the inside than the outside had led her to believe. In some ways, it was worse.

The interior was smaller than it looked and there were only two light switches—one for each floor—located in the living and bedroom respectively. The lower floor consisted of the kitchen and living room, bisected by a bar-style counter. A very steep and narrow staircase, carpeted in bright orange shag, led up to a bedroom barely big enough for the full-sized bed it housed and a tiny closet of a bathroom. The unexpected marriage of old and new appliances was something straight out of Hayseeds-R-Us. A claw-foot tub and pull-string toilet waged an aesthetics war with the faux-Grecian pedestal sink and camouflage shower curtain, complete with deer heads poking out at odd angles. A chipped, rusted and very old medicine cabinet hung off-centered on the only wall wide enough to occupy it, and that was over the tub, not the sink.

    The entire cabin, both upstairs and down, couldn't have been more than six hundred square feet. It was sparsely furnished, mostly clean (apart from a little dust) and haunted in the corners by cobwebs. That no one had lived here in quite some time was obvious. Now she did.

    Welcome home.

    Karly shivered.

CHAPTER TWO

The dog stood in the center of the bathtub with his head hanging low, his tail tucked and his yellow eyes locked on her face. His was a canine expression that held all the subtle nuances of 'Why me?' and 'Lady, what did I ever do to you?'

Karly bathed him anyway. Her gentle fingers probed through thick black fur, searching for injuries her eyes couldn't seem to verify, but which she knew had to be there. Admittedly, she wasn't a veterinarian. She'd never owned a pet before—not as a child and certainly not as an adult—but that didn't stop her from touching every inch of him. She ran her hands up and down his limbs, over his ribs, along his spine all the way to the tip of his drooping tail. Nothing felt broken or swollen, and the dog neither flinched nor yelped. Ultimately, she figured he'd probably be all right once his bumps and bruises, sore muscles, and scratches had a chance to heal.

The worst injury she could find was on his back leg, the one he'd been lying on in the car (as the crimson smears clearly attested). His entire right flank was matted with blood, but once she'd softened it with a little soap and warm water, patiently working the mat loose to part the thick black fur, all she found was the smallest of cuts. It wasn't even bleeding anymore.

"There's a good puppy." She gave him a pat and turned the water off. "You're going to be okay."

Head and tail both hanging, the dog stayed exactly as she'd left him while she found a towel and wrapped it around him. He didn't even try to shake himself off.

"Poor baby." He must be one hurting puppy. She dried him gently, giving liberal scritches behind his ears, and did her very best not to make it all feel worse.

His fur was very long and held a lot of water. It took two towels to get him to a point where he wasn't dripping a lake's worth of water into the bottom of the tub.

"Come on." Hanging the towels up over the curtain rod, she stepped away from the tub. "Can you get out by yourself?"

He looked at her, tail still tucked—wet, sore and miserable.

She opened the bathroom door to make it a little more obvious that the punishment was over. "Come on, puppy," she coaxed. "Paroling all prisoners."

The dog looked from her to the door, and then shuffled closer to the edge of the tub. He crawled out one paw at a time with soft chuffing groans following each hobbling step. He looked so stiff and sore.

"What a brave boy." She offered another sympathetic pat. "Come on, I think I've got an aspirin in my purse."

She made her way downstairs, moving slowly and looking back often to see if he was still following. He was. Each step every bit as stiff and deliberate as when he'd followed her up and into the bathroom. She found a dish in the cupboard, which she filled with cool water and put down on the floor near the wall so he could drink. He didn't. He hobbled only as far as it took for kitchen linoleum to meet garish orange carpet and then he stopped, and stood there, staring while she started dinner.

Generic hamburger helper never smelled so good, although that might have been because she was incredibly hungry. She hadn't eaten all day, not since before Dan had come barreling home with those divorce papers clutched in one hand and his other clenched in a tight fist. It wouldn't have mattered how they'd been delivered to him, but that they were delivered at work in front of all his cop buddies, and just minutes before she'd been ready to run…

She touched her bruised eye, prodding tenderly, fully aware of how much worse it could have been. From the corner of her good eye, she saw those yellow eyes watching her. "I guess we've both taken our lumps today, huh? I'm very sorry about giving you yours."

He hobbled a step closer, his sharp nails clicking on the linoleum. He looked from her to the stove, to the bowl of water, and back to her again. She really ought to find that aspirin and see if she couldn't ease his discomfort.

Stirring the brown beef and noodles together, she left the mixture to simmer and picked up her purse, still on the counter where she'd dropped it along with the supplies she'd picked up at the local store. She found a small bottle of aspirin at the bottom under her keys, and shook two pills out into her hand. One she broke in half, setting a partial piece to one side while she took the other herself. With a spoon, she fished a larger clump of hamburger from the pan. Blowing until it cooled, she tucked the partial dose into it and offered it to the motionless dog.

He did not shy from her. Apart from rotating his ears toward her, he didn't move at all.

"Look what I have for you," she coaxed, dropping to one knee. She held the aspirin-laced hamburger out in her open palm. "Yummy ground beef. Ninety-three percent lean. Nothing but the best for puppies I hit with the car. Come on, take it."

His lupine gaze never left her face. But after a moment, one stiff step at a time, the dog came closer. He stared eerily deep into her eyes for a very long time before, with another soft groan—almost like a sigh of defeat—he ate the meat from her palm. He took it gently, his sharp teeth never touching her skin, and then stood in meek acceptance of the cautious, two-fingered scratch she bestowed on top of his massive head.

"There's a good boy," Karly murmured, petting him. "Such a handsome puppy."

And he was, too. Having never had one before, Karly knew next to nothing about dogs. She knew enough to recognize a wiener dog from a hot dog, and that was about it—the total extent of her canine familiarity. Her basic animal knowledge went a little further and included tidbit gems like: if it has teeth, it can bite you. And, injured animals probably shouldn't be fed hamburger helper by hand. But this one seemed rather sweet, his mannerisms bringing to mind old gentlemen in furry tuxedoes.

Somewhere in the growing darkness outside the cabin, a long, low howl cut the night.

Puppy's ears swiveled, tracking the sound, but otherwise he didn't move. Startled, Karly went to steal a peek out through the small window above the kitchen sink. She craned her neck while her breath fogged the glass, but all she could see were shadows and trees, waving gently in the passing of a stiff wind.

The howl came again, low and mournful, shivering its way up her spine because it didn't sound as if it were very far away at all. A moment later, it was echoed by another more distant voice and then, quite suddenly, by a third that was right in the very room with her. Karly spun, staring in shock as Puppy, head tipped up and muzzle extended, sang back. Those mournful notes sent tiny, icy fingers positively scampering up and down her spine, raising every fine hair on her body until all she could feel was the prickle as they stood upright.

Wolf.

It was the first word that leapt right to the forefront of Karly's mind. She'd seen a movie about those once, too—*Never Cry Wolf* starring Charles Martin Smith. Damn fine actor. She couldn't remember a single thing about the film apart from Smith catching and eating a lot of mice, and yet as she stood there, staring at the massive dog singing so loudly and so desolately not four feet away, suddenly wolves were very much at the forefront of her mind.

Which was silly. Dogs howled, too. Everybody knew dogs howled—even *bona fide* city girls like her knew dogs howled. Barks, yips and baying could be heard for miles around every time the sirens went off, be it an ambulance, fire truck or police car. At two in the afternoon or two in the morning, it didn't matter. When the sirens went whizzing past Redemption suburbia, every dog in the neighborhood sounded the alarm, but not one of them had ever sounded like this.

A fact that did not automatically make this particular dog a wolf, she told herself firmly. A wolf would never have allowed her to get close enough to roll him in her coat. He wouldn't have let her put him in the back of her car, or bathe him in her bathroom, or eaten out of the palm of her hand as sweetly as Puppy had. And if all that weren't proof enough that this big, black, shaggy beast standing in her kitchen could not possibly be a wolf, there was still Margo. Margo had told her to watch out for the animals, not wolves. Knowing all of that, however, did not make listening to this any less…eerie.

The howling abruptly ceased, both inside the tiny cabin and out. Lowering his head, Puppy looked at her again with those yellow, yellow eyes. Everything was quiet. Painfully quiet. All she could hear was the sizzling of their supper on the stove and the pounding of her nervous heart.

"Please don't do that again," she whispered, uneasy.

Puppy neither blinked nor looked away, and made no promises.

With a pained groan, he eased himself into a sit and then pointedly shifted his stare to the stove where their supper was now burning.

Karly leapt to rescue it, yanking the pan off the heat and quickly stirring to keep what was on the bottom from scorching any worse than it already had. By the time she'd turned around again, Puppy was lying down with his massive black head resting on his massive black paws, looking completely doglike once more.

Which, of course, he should since that was what he was—a dog.

Just an ordinary, everyday, bushy-haired, yellow-eyed, occasionally very wolfish-seeming dog.

* * * * *

Country quiet was as different from city quiet as earth was from sky. In the city, quiet meant fewer cars on the roads, less honking, less shouting and fewer jacked up radios or TVs in the middle of the night. In the country, Karly found, quiet was so far removed from what she was familiar with as to make it a completely different animal altogether.

Quiet was horrible in its unfamiliarity. Sporadic whispers of wind made the branches of the surrounding trees tap at the cabin's roof and walls and scratch at the kitchen window like a serial killer itching for entry. There was an entire forest's worth of crickets out there—she'd never heard such a racket in her life. The constant chirping somehow echoed out into the moonless, starlit black night, so soft and yet so deafening. And the owls. There was one somewhere just outside her bedroom window and every few seconds it let loose a deep *hoo-hoohoohoo-hooooo!*—a rhythmic and ever-changing Morse code of hoots that just about caused her to jump straight out of her skin.

Curled up on her side, it was a fight not to cry. Karly had dreamed of this for almost four years: her first night of total freedom away from Dan, the lectures, the guilt and blame and beatings. If she'd had any idea how much more terrifying this all would be, she never would have run.

And there it was again, the scariest sound of all: the dog—not Puppy this time, but the one right outside her house. Chuffing, whining, skulking around the foundation of the cabin and rustling through the bushes. Toe claws clicked over both front and back porches as every window and door was thoroughly investigated. Now and then, she could even hear the snuffling as a black nose pressed up against every crack, taking careful note of her. She'd never been so terrified in her life.

Lying between the faintly must-smelling sheets, Karly clutched at her pillow, listened intently for the inevitable sounds of that beast finally just breaking in. She wanted to go home. Even knowing the beating that waited for her, if she'd thought for a second she could make it to her car, she'd have fled.

But she wouldn't make it. Within steps of opening her front door, the beast hunting in the shadows out there was going to get her, she was sure of it. She was trapped here, in this strange house, in this awful wilderness.

How could she have been so stupid? Had life with Dan really been so bad? Yes, of course it had, but how could she have thought *this* would be any better?

A single hot tear trickled past her lashes and Karly knuckled it away. Unfortunately, that small escape was enough to break the dam, and the rest she let soak into her pillow, turning the fabric hot and wet beneath her cheek. Staring fixedly into the darkness, she made herself small and quiet, breathing as softly as she could through her open mouth so the creatures outside wouldn't hear her. After so many years with Dan, survival had made her an expert in the art of crying soundlessly.

The snuffling had moved around to the back of the house, now. The owl on the roof loosed another stream of rapid-fire hoots. And just outside her bedroom door, a carpet-muffled floorboard creaked. Karly snapped up off her pillow, every nerve inside her crawling with dread as she stared back over her shoulder, but it was only Puppy.

His shadowed silhouette barely distinguishable from the rest of the black, he nosed open her bedroom door and stood there, watching her for several long minutes before slipping inside. Soft padding steps rounded the end of the bed, but she didn't see him again until he crossed between her and the faintly lighter darkness of the world outside her window. Hooking his muzzle over the mattress, he studied her.

"It's okay," she whispered, her voice shaky with the tears she couldn't quite keep back. She patted the mattress. "Do you want to sleep with me? I don't mind company."

He made a sound then, the first audible thing she'd heard from him since that awful howl in the kitchen. Groaning, he climbed up onto the bed beside her.

The warm tip of his nose touched her chin, her cheek, her hair. He lapped away a falling tear and then lay down beside her. Big as he was, he filled the mattress, but Karly didn't care. She made room for him, allowing him the lion's share before scooting in close. She curled against him, weaving her fingers into all that soft, thick fur and holding on tight for comfort.

"You won't let anything get me, will you, Puppy?" She felt him breathe in, the massive chest beneath her fingers lifting before deflating again in a contented sigh.

She really was stupid. He was just a dog—an injured one, at that. And yet, already she felt safer.

* * * * *

He never should have gotten into bed with her.

Lying stiff and still, Colton stared at the stars shining in through the single bedroom window and tried not to let the kneading grip of the woman's small hands get to him. He knew better than this. He never would have come upstairs at all, except that he'd heard her crying. Battered women, they were his weakness and always had been, all the way back to the woman who'd given birth to him.

He didn't have time for this. He should have stayed downstairs, kept his distance, and snuck out hours ago. It didn't matter what her trouble was. She wasn't *volka*. He could smell the humanness of her with every sigh he tried to smother. Not only was she *chelovak*, but she wasn't even from Hollow Hills. Hell, no resident non-*volka* would have come racing up these back roads like she had. And he'd crawled into bed with her, laid down as if they were friends, and let her put her arms around him and cuddle in close.

Her tears were in his fur. He could feel the hitch of every sob she took in the brush of her breasts against his back. The urge to transform right here, to roll over, wrap his arms around her and simply offer comfort was every bit as strong as his need to get up and leave. He couldn't afford to lie here all night. He had a Hunt to prepare for, early arrivers to welcome in, and a presence of authority to establish if he wanted his position as Alpha to be taken seriously. Where in all of that was there time for this?

Behind him, those hitching gasps and shuddering breaths were dwindling. Her weeping eased first, followed by her trembling and those tiny clutching motions she kept making against the scruff of his neck. Colton remained as if frozen until he was certain the woman had cried herself into an exhausted sleep. Then and only then, did he try to disentangle himself from her clinging grip.

He moved slowly, slipping off the mattress by careful degrees, each subtle movement loosening her grip until her hands fell limp from his fur onto the sheets and finally he was free to crawl out of bed. She whimpered once and he looked back. But when she only burrowed deeper into her pillow, he padded silently back across the carpet and left the room.

He was stiff and he was sore, but as far as car accidents went he'd gotten off easy. At least nothing felt broken and he didn't feel so bad as to suspect internal bleeding. Given a couple days, he'd recover, and a couple days was all he needed to make sure the Hunt went the way he needed it to. The way Hollow Hills needed it to.

If, that is, he survived these stairs...

Colton stood in the hallway, gazing down into the living room below. His pack brother was calling to him, scratching at the cracks around the doors, prowling the cabin's perimeter in search of a quiet way in, and he dreaded—absolutely dreaded—having to take that first descending step. He growled, but the stairs were unrelenting and there was no avoiding it. Going down was going to hurt.

Pain was good, as his father used to say. It meant he was still alive.

God, he hadn't thought about that sonofabitch in years.

One aching step at a time, Colton made his way to the living room floor. He could already hear his pack brother pacing restlessly on the front porch, quivering nose pulling his scent from the crack beneath the door. It was an old cabin with an old door. The sliding bolt was easy to push back, even in wolf form, and once he had it unlocked, his pack brother immediately spilled inside.

He greeted Colton with muted whines and submissive posturing, nosing at him from muzzle to flank as he was checked for injury. Colton waited patiently, letting him take stock of every wound, as well as the scent of the woman clinging to his fur just like her hands had done. He tried not to think about it. He didn't look back either, not when he stepped off the front porch and certainly not when he led his pack brother, who fell into obedient step at his flank, back across the yard toward the trees.

He itched to turn around and see if she was watching him go from that little upstairs window, but he didn't. There was no earthly reason for why he should feel pulled toward a *chelovak,* one he didn't even know. Hell, one who had hit him with her car!

His muscles flexed and his flanks rippled, equal parts irritation and unease as he felt again the soft grip of her fingers plucking at his fur. Her fear and uncertainty were still in his nose; he could smell it on the cool evening air. He owed her nothing, but just as he neared the wooded edge of the yard, he hesitated.

His pack brother paused, ears perking when Colton abruptly turned back. He patrolled the cabin's exterior, marking both the front and back doors and her car. This was one of Mama Margo's cabins, habitually rented to outsiders. There weren't many in Hollow Hills foolish enough to actively court the old woman's wrath by hassling one of her visiting *chelovak.* Still, with the McQueens just down the road, it paid to be cautious, so he left his scent everywhere.

Trusting that to be enough for now, he rejoined his pack of one and let the allure of the night's pleasures as well as its responsibilities draw him away.

CHAPTER THREE

Karly dreamt about wolves, but when she awoke in the morning, she couldn't remember any of it apart from the eerie howls that had plagued her throughout the night. All of that was gone now though. The house was painfully quiet and the morning sun shone in through the split in the bedroom curtains, splashing light across her face, the best of all possible alarm clocks. Rolling over did little to help escape it. Every corner of her new bedroom was brightly lit, and in the end, all Karly could do was admit defeat. She reached sleepily across the bed, but when her hand encountered only empty mattress, she opened her eyes.

The dog was gone. She was alone.

"Puppy?" Karly sat up in bed, listening carefully, but no hint of answering movement sounded from anywhere in the cabin.

Had he died in the night? Oh God. Crawling across the mattress, she checked the floor on the far side, but Puppy wasn't there either. She got up. Small as the cabin was, it took only a few minutes of searching and one glance at the open front door for her to realize what had happened. The dog really was gone. Apparently, he'd let himself out through the front door.

Bare feet padding from carpet to cool floorboards, Karly slipped out onto the porch. Dressed in only her nightshirt, she hugged herself against the early morning chill as she searched the yard.

"Puppy!" Feigning a cheerful whistle, Karly clapped her hands twice. "Come on, baby!"

Not a single bush rustled and no big, black, wolfish canine stuck his head out into the open to look at her.

Maybe he'd gone home. He wasn't really her dog, after all. He probably had a family, people who'd searched or worried about him all night long because of her.

Karly made a face, trying not to feel so disappointed. She wasn't really a dog person anyway.

Sweeping the wooded landscape with one last hopeful glance, she went back inside. She almost closed the door but then, just on the off chance, left it open and went upstairs.

Unpacking what few belongings she had from her suitcase into the two-drawer chest at the foot of her bed took all of about three minutes, and then only because she had to refold everything first. She found a safe place to stash her money can under the bed (the unoriginality of that plan was not lost on her) and then gathered her things for a shower. Wandering into the bathroom, she searched the wall for the light switch, but nothing happened when she flicked it on. Glancing up at the naked bulb, she flicked the switch up and down several times with the same lack of results.

Downstairs, the kitchen was the same. Her cellphone was still on its charger on the kitchen counter where she'd left it last night, but although fully charged now, the electrical outlet was every bit as dead as the lights. She looked out the window, but the weather was sunny as sunny could be.

Biting her bottom lip, Karly circled the small kitchen, wondering where the fuse box was, unsure if she knew how to fix a blown fuse or even if she'd recognize one if she saw it. Should she call Margo? Should she call the power company?

Her stomach tightened. If she called the power company and made a report, was that something Dan could use to track her by? Maybe she didn't have power because he already knew where she was. What if he was waiting for her outside right now? What if she had no power because he'd cut the lines just to scare her?

As if on cue, she heard the grinding crunch of tires rolling up the unpaved road just outside, and Karly nearly stopped breathing. Her chest seized, every muscle she had lurching into clumsy motion as she ran to the front door and quickly slammed it shut. Through a narrow part in the living room window curtains, she watched the shiny white hood and silver bumper of a police truck drive right up to her front porch before easing to a gentle stop, just feet from the railing.

That Dan had never driven a white, marked police truck (as far as she was aware) never even figured into it. She still threw all her weight against the old door, her fingers fumbling with the sliding bolt, jerking, shoving, yanking, and finally slapping frantically until it locked into place. There she stayed, on the verge of hysterics, feet braced against the floor to press as much of herself as she could against the old wood.

As if that would stop Dan from breaking in.

He was going to kill her. He was absolutely going to kill her, and there was no one around to stop him and no one that she could call for help. Sinking with dread, all Karly could do was listen as the truck came to a gravel-crunching stop outside her window. Both truck doors opened and then lightly slammed shut. Twin footsteps approached the porch. Only one ascended though—slow, heavy-tromping boots making their way to stand where a welcome mat would have been, had she owned one. Just this old door, locked with a flimsy sliding bolt, stood between them.

Three steady knocks made her jump. "Hello, anybody home?"

It took her almost three fully-panicked heartbeats before she realize that was not Dan's voice. That didn't mean he wasn't standing silently right outside or that the owner of that perfectly nice sounding voice wasn't one of his cop buddies. She held herself frozen, one hand locked over her mouth to stifle any inadvertent sounds. She closed her eyes, praying they both would just go away.

Seconds crawled into a minute. Quite possibly, the longest of her life.

Another brisk knock rapped the opposite side of the door, a little louder this time. "Ms. Smith, are you in there?"

"Want me to check around back?" another man asked. He wasn't Dan either.

"Yeah, but make some noise. Margo said not to spook her."

Margo sent them? Trembling, Karly opened her eyes. She stared at the door, but didn't move. Every inch of her remained pressed hard against the slats.

One set of footsteps retreated back off the porch to crunch through the gravel, brush and leaves as they circled around the side of the small cabin; the owner of the other set stayed behind. It was probably a figment of her fear, but in the terrible silence that followed, she thought she heard him draw a breath. In and of itself, that certainly wasn't strange. Except that from the sound of it, she would have sworn he must have had his nose right up against the wood. He inhaled slowly, pulling in all the scented air filling up the cracks between the slats of the wooden door. There was no reason for why he would do that, though. Only in the overactive imagination of a terrified mind could such a thing make logical sense.

She tried to calm down, but then the man on her front porch began to move.

"Don't be afraid," he said, as he began to drift towards the living room window. He spoke softly, as if he knew not only that she was right there, but that she could hear him. That she was afraid of him.

Karly followed the sounds of his footsteps across the porch. The curtains of that window were open just a crack, but that crack was wide enough to betray her. When his shadow passed over it, hands cupped against the glass to peek inside, Karly flattened her back against the slats and tried to slip deeper into the corner where the door and wall joined. Hung on hinges quite possibly as old as the cabin, the door rattled when her weight shifted. It was only the slightest of sounds, but it froze her instantly. It also gave her away.

The shadow of his head turned. A moment later, those slow footsteps and the soft, deep voice came back to the door. "It's okay, Miss Smith. I'm no one you need fear."

Karly held her breath, but the cause was already lost. He knew she was here.

"My name is Colton Lauren." His tone low and soothing, the man on the porch spoke to her through the door. "I'm with Fish and Game. Would you mind opening the door?"

Fish and Game? Although close enough to almost make no difference, at least he wasn't police. The knots in her stomach loosened a bit. She shifted uncertainly, still braced against the door in case he tried to force his way inside.

"I'm not poaching anything," she said shakily, and made no move to unlock the sliding latch.

"No, ma'am." She could hear his smile in his voice. "I never said you were. Margo sent us. Can you open the door?"

She didn't move. "Why?"

"No official reason," he assured. "But it would make passing this food basket a little easier."

A moving shadow beyond the kitchen window caught the corner of her eye. Karly glanced back to find the other man, also a warden by the tan color of his uniform, with his face pressed to the glass of the rear door and hands cupped around his eyes to block the glare. He waved at her with the fingers of one.

"Morning," he called. Pulling back from the door, the warden tipped his head and shouted around the house, "She's home, Cole!"

She heard the stifled sigh and then the humor in Colton Lauren's voice when he called back, "Yeah. Thanks, Gabe. I'm talking to her now."

Karly shifted again, feeling awkward and scared, but a little silly now, too. With a shaky hand, she reached for the latch, hesitating twice before sliding it back. She braced her foot against the bottom of the door, preventing it from opening more than an inch or two, and peeked outside. There was no helping that she looked out at him black eye first. That was just the way the door opened, and she wanted to keep that barrier (even if the hinges were rusty and the wood old) between them.

"Morning." Colton Lauren looked down at her with amber eyes that probably didn't miss much and smiled. He was tall, broad in the shoulders, lean and muscular in a way that bespoke of active living rather than a gym membership. His hair was dark, his skin the golden color of someone who spent a lot of time in the sun, and his honeyed gaze stayed locked with hers. He took in the visible bruise without comment, though he did lower himself to prop one shoulder against the jamb. It dropped him down to eye level with her, but if he was trying to make himself seem less threatening, it didn't work. Experience was a hard teacher. Hers had taught her that men were dangerous, no matter how they first appeared.

"What basket?" she finally asked. "I didn't order anything."

He shifted, bringing the picnic basket he held in one hand around where she could see it. "Compliments of Mama Margo. A couple fishermen imbibed a bit too freely last night and ran their truck head-on into an electric pole. Half of Hollow Hills is without power. Montgomery Municipal sent someone out, but that doesn't mean we'll get power back any time soon. She thought you might like something to eat, seeing as how you're new here and might not have anything."

"Margo is your mom?"

His full mouth tipped into an easy smile. "As good as, though not by birth. I guess you could say she takes in all sorts of strays." He held up the basket, tempting her to open the door a little wider. "It's nothing special. A couple sandwiches, some fruit…a piece of her award-winning apple pie. Literally. County fair, three years running now. Buttery crust so delicate it'll melt in your mouth. If you don't want it, Gabe and I'll have no problem polishing those sandwiches off, but we'll have to wrestle for the pie, being as there's only one slice." Those honey-colored eyes twinkled down into hers. "I'm pretty sure I can take him."

His smile was beguiling. The knots in her stomach begged her not to trust him, but after only a moment, Karly slid her foot aside and opened the door wide enough to take the basket. She moved slowly. He remained non-threatening.

"Thank you," she whispered.

"No problem." Relieved of the basket, he tapped two knuckles against the threshold, then pushed backwards off it. "You have a good day, now. Welcome to Hollow Hills."

The other Fish and Game officer, Gabe, came around the side of the house. He tossed Karly a smile, touching a two-fingered salute to the brim of his hat. She didn't smile back; she simply closed the door. It was immediately locked again.

Hugging the basket to her nervous stomach, Karly crept close enough to the living room window to watch as the wardens sauntered back to their truck. They were talking, but their voices were too low for her to make out any words. The men crossed paths at the bumper. Colton glanced back once at the cabin, causing her to flinch back into the shadows, before he got in behind the steering wheel. It took a three-point turn for him to maneuver the truck out of her little cul-de-sac of a driveway and then they were back on the dirt road and driving away.

Karly watched until the truck was completely gone and the dry dust of the dirt road had settled once more. Still hugging the basket, she went into the kitchen and sat at the small table. She didn't eat right away. Nervous as she was, she was afraid she'd throw up if she tried. She just sat there, for the longest time, thinking about Puppy and Margo.

Colton seemed very nice, too. Not that it mattered.

She doubted if she'd ever trust another man again. It just wasn't worth the risk.

* * * * *

Colton drove with one hand on the wheel and one elbow hanging out the driver's side window. He rubbed his mouth, thinking, and what he was thinking did not make him happy.

Her eye looked worse today than he remembered it, but then, morning-after black eyes usually did. So, it was that fresh. Someone had hit her yesterday. Judging by that haunted look she'd worn, someone had hit her more than once.

His hand tightened on the steering wheel.

She's running, Mama Margo had said. *Go and make your acquaintance so she'll know who to go running to.*

At the time she'd said it, her request had annoyed him a little, but now...his hand tightened even more. He despised bullies and men who beat on the women they should be protecting. He shook his head, already feeling that rock hardness tightening in his gut, spreading out cold before the heat of the oncoming shift tempted him. He didn't need to check the rearview mirror to know the honeyed amber of his eyes was turning gold. Going wolf.

He swallowed back the urge. He had too much to do, too many responsibilities pulling at him to do this now. And over a woman he didn't know? He rubbed his mouth again. He didn't need this. Not now.

From the passenger seat, Gabe eyed him cautiously. "What are you thinking?"

He was thinking about his mother, hiding her own blackened eyes with her hair while they cowered under the basement steps, jumping at every crashing slam as his father raged through the house in his search for her.

"Nothing," Coleton said, and tried to flash Gabe a poor imitation of his normal, everyday, easy-going smile. His knuckles on the steering wheel were white.

"Okay." Gabe looked from Colton's hands back to his face. "Does this mean we're going up to North Ridge now?"

"Yup." But Colton glanced in the rearview mirror when he said it. The trees had swallowed up the rental cabin. He couldn't see it anymore and yet he couldn't stop seeing her, the way she'd tried to tuck herself behind that rickety old door, a rabbit on the verge of bolting.

"Good." Gabe looked him over carefully, before apparently deciding to accept him at his word. "Good!" He nodded, then grinned, his hands patting out a rhythm on his knees. "Let's get our heads back in the game, then."

"Right."

"You won't believe some of the ladies who have turned up for the Hunt this year. We are talking fine, fine, *fine* females. Even better, Maya's mama told Margo she's planning to join up."

"Maya's mama is already mated."

"I'm talking about Maya, and you damn well know it." Gabe's flash of irritation faded and his hands stilled on his knees. "What I wouldn't give to be the one to catch her. Have you looked into her eyes, Cole? God, she's got the most incredible eyes."

Colton barely heard him. All he could think about were bruise-rimmed baby blues staring out at him through the crack in the door—

"I swear," Gabe continued, casting a soft smile out the passenger window. "Maya can look right through a man and just…stop his heart mid-beat. Have you ever seen eyes like that before?"

—*Karly Smith, curled up next to him in her bed last night, her small hands pulling at his fur, jumping at every sound, crying herself to sleep—*

"Cole?"

What kind of man would do that, take a woman he professed to love and break her down that way? A man like his father, that's what kind.

Coleton grit his teeth, trying to keep back the canines itching to lengthen.

"Okay," Gabe suddenly said. "What are we doing now?"

It wasn't until then that Colton realized he'd stopped the truck. They were idling in the middle of the narrow dirt road with his white-knuckled grip anchoring him to the steering wheel the way her white-knuckled grip had anchored into his fur last night.

The *chelovak* was pulling at him and he didn't know why. She wasn't his mother, his sister, his lover; she wasn't even a member of his pack. But she had run to Hollow Hills and this was his territory. In a roundabout way, that made her his, the same way every man, woman and child became his when he'd stepped into the vacant Alpha position.

His…

His belly heated, pulled. Tightened.

Shifting into park, Colton popped his seatbelt and got out of the truck. For the first time in his life, he actually found himself feeling grateful for the ill-tempered, gun-toting McQueens. He looked up and down the road, but there wasn't another car in sight. Unless some out-of-town fisherman was roaming lost in these old hills, he wasn't likely to be seen.

"Cole?" Gabe tried again as Colton began to strip out of his clothes.

"I'm going back," Colton said, shortly.

"Why?"

No reason. Every reason. Hell, he didn't know.

"Call it gut instinct. Margo was right; I think our Miss Smith is running. And if she is, that means trouble's probably following her. I want to know what that trouble is."

"What do you want to bet her name isn't even Smith?"

"That's a bet I wouldn't take." Colton kicked off his boots, stuffed his socks down into the toes and tossed them into the back of the pickup. His uniform shirt, he tucked into the cab behind the driver's seat. Looking warily up and down the road again, he unbuckled his belt.

"What am I supposed to tell people when you don't come to the Ridge for a Hunt you offered to host, for the express purpose of bagging yourself a Bride? The pack has to grow, Cole. The two of us, we're good. But we won't hold this territory another year if we don't."

"Don't tell me what I already know," Colton snapped, the same flush of irritation hitting him that he felt every time he had to think about this. He was the Alpha. An Alpha did what he had to for the good of the pack and that included finding a Bride and building their numbers. Brides for an Alpha and his lieutenants meant stability gained through other pack ties. Pups meant permanence, and until he gained that, he would never have the complete loyalty or support of the ferine residents of Hollow Hills'. Or the respect of other potential Alphas, like Sebastian McQueen and his brothers, all of whom harbored ambitions for stepping into his place if he failed.

Colton bristled. Over his dead body. Hot-headed males who talked with violence first and common sense later were not what Hollow Hills needed.

"Seventeen females have turned out already," Gabe continued. "*Seventeen*. At least twenty-two males joined the roster to run for them, with another four days to accrue more." He was quiet a moment. "The McQueens registered, too. All four of them."

"I'll be there for the Hunt."

"You'd better be there for the pre-games," Gabe said wryly. "You *have* to be. If they seduce one Bride, just one who's willing to let them catch her and we don't, then we're done. We'll either be showing our throats to Sebastian or we'll have to find someplace else to live."

"I know what's at stake," Colton muttered, and shucked out of both his pants and his underwear. Wadding them in a ball, he threw them behind the seat as well.

"Do you?" Glaring back at him, Gabe got out of the truck and came around to the driver's side. "Then prove it. In four days, your head had better be out of that cabin, off that woman—that *chelovak* woman, who hit you with her car, I might add—and back up on the Ridge where it belongs, or else."

Colton blinked twice, almost amused when his normally mild-mannered lieutenant shouldered past him and stepped up into the truck. "Or else what, Gabe?"

"Or else I'm taking over the pack and finding myself a new best friend." Gabe flashed him a grin that didn't quite reach as far as his somber eyes.

"You're lucky I don't just give it to you," Colton replied, but it was a bluff and they both knew it.

Standing naked in the road, Colton watched the truck drive off. He frowned, knowing he ought to be up on that Ridge, putting in a strong appearance while wooing females, attracting lone *volka* males looking to stop wandering and put down roots, and soundly beating his rivals in pre-Hunt games that would show everyone just how young, strong and in his physical prime he truly was. But his gut was pulling him in the opposite direction and, after a moment, he gave in to it.

Colton turned, shifting even as he began to run, back up the road toward Margo's rental cabin and the last woman in town that he should be paying attention to right now.

CHAPTER FOUR

As the minutes passed and the Fish and Game—police, she had to remind herself; just like Dan, only in slightly different uniforms—failed to return, Karly let herself relax. Eventually, she even stopped hugging the basket. She'd held onto it so tightly one side was crushed beneath her arm. Not wanting to return it to Margo in anything less than perfect condition, she placed the basket on the table and quietly unpacked the contents to see if she could press it back into shape.

She found the pie first. It was right on top, with an orange and a couple of bananas underneath. On the very bottom were two sandwiches. Very simple bologna and cheese, wrapped in cellophane for freshness. She was about to open one when she heard a faint whine followed by scratching at the front door.

Karly ran to let Puppy in, surprised at how happy it made her just to see him moving so well. He sauntered across the threshold, ears alert and tail lazily wagging. "There you are! Where have you been? You missed the excitement. We had visitors."

She couldn't help glancing back down the road, but the officers and their truck were well and truly gone. That made her feel better too.

She closed and locked the door anyway. "Ready for breakfast?"

He followed her to the kitchen where she broke one of the sandwiches in half and offered him the larger piece.

"Come on," she coaxed when he only looked at it. "It's not the Ritz, but it's what we've got. We'll go shopping in a—"

Her cellphone rang. Knots seized her insides, strangling so tightly for a moment Karly couldn't breathe. She got up to check the number. Only half those knots eased when she recognized it. It definitely wasn't Dan.

Putting her sandwich down, she picked up the phone and by way of 'hello' said, "I'm out."

"Good," Beth Calloway, her lawyer—and as far as Karly was concerned, the best damn lawyer in the world—replied. "How far did you get?"

"All the way across state lines. I'm in Hollow Hills. I'm renting a place from a very nice lady who's willing to keep the utilities in her name."

"How are you for money?"

"I've got everything mama left me." She choked a little at that. "I'll be okay for a while. How long do you think he's going to look for me?"

"You would know that better than I would. However, I do have some good news in that department. For one, your husband has already signed the divorce papers. They were delivered by courier first thing this morning."

Stunned, Karly stared across the kitchen at nothing. "He's not contesting anything?"

"No, and Karly—" Caution weighed heavy in her lawyer's tone. "I've never had an abuser let go this easily. Has he tried to contact you?"

"No, not yet." Karly rubbed her suddenly sweaty palms against her thighs. She looked down when she felt a nose nudge under her wrist. When Puppy ducked under her hand to rest his chin on top of her leg, she petted him instead. "He got a parting shot though. I've one real killer of a black eye."

"Can you get a hold of a newspaper with today's date on it?"

"I don't know. Probably."

"Use your new cellphone to take a picture of it and any other fresh bruises alongside the newspaper, Be sure the date shows, and send them to me. I'll add them to your dossier, just in case. He's not contesting anything right now, but that doesn't mean he won't later on just to make things difficult for you."

"I'm not asking for anything. I just want out."

"I know, but that doesn't mean he won't look for ways to drag this out and punish you further. I don't know that he will. He might not even try. I don't think he wants all his cop buddies to know he beats his wife. That's our wild card, and he'd better believe I'll play it and go after everything he has—house, truck, boat, almost twenty grand in that savings account he's trying so damn hard to hide at First Federal, his pension and his retirement—if he pushes me."

"He has an account at First Federal?" What else did he have that she didn't know about? Her stomach twisted into a hard knot of unease.

"Yes, and a lock box. God only knows what he's hiding in that. A friend of mine in the Department told me Dan took the rest of the week off. If he's smart, he'll spend it hiring a lawyer and getting his act together, but no one's contacted me yet. Still, I thought you ought to know. Keep your head down and be careful. Don't change your driver's license, don't register your car, and whatever you do, don't get pulled over for speeding. Do get me those pictures as soon as you can, preferably while the marks are still fresh and ugly. And do make a friend or two where you are now—someone who'll keep an eye out for you."

"I will," Karly promised, burying her fingers in Puppy's soft fur and drawing what comfort she could from his warmth pressed against her leg. She had no idea who that friend might be. Margo maybe. Mama Margo, they'd called her. Yeah, she could probably trust Margo.

Beth's voice softened. "I can still get you into that shelter, Karly. You've done nothing to be ashamed of, and they're very good at what they do. They can hide you in places Dan would never—"

"No." Karly lifted her chin, shaking her head even though Beth couldn't see it. For the first time in four long years, she had reclaimed her freedom. She wasn't about to give it up again for any reason. "Thank you, but no. I...I'm going to be all right."

She said it as if it were true. She even said it as if she believed it.

"You're the boss," Beth finally said. "I just want you to know the option is there if you need it."

"That's okay." She looked down at Puppy, who looked boldly back up at her. His yellow eyes bored into hers, his ears perked as if he weren't just listening, but also understood. Almost against her will, Karly smiled. "I'll be fine. As it turns out, I've already got a protector." Snapping her phone closed, Karly set the phone aside. She cupped Puppy's furry muzzle between her hands, losing her fingers in the soft black of his fur as she stroked his massive head. "You've got more teeth than Dan does, don't you, Puppy? You won't let anything happen to me, will you, boy?"

Thumping his tail twice against the floor, he met her eyes without blinking and did not look away.

Comforted, she stroked his soft face again and then got up. "Finish your breakfast. We've got a busy day ahead of us."

Because he was such a big dog, she gave Puppy the remaining sandwich while she made do with a banana and the smaller half of that first sandwich. Seeming reluctant to eat at first, it wasn't until she lay half of Margo's award-winning pie in front of him that Puppy gave in to chop-licking temptation. Karly was just hungry enough to eat the second banana too, but set the orange in the fridge for later and, while Puppy contented himself with licking up every last bit of the apple pie she'd given him, she went upstairs.

Fishing her cashbox out from under her bed, Karly counted out a cautious sum and then hid the rest again. Back downstairs, she gave Puppy a scratch behind the ears as she put the dishes in the sink for later. Gathering her cellphone and her purse, she fished the car keys from one of the pockets and, with Puppy riding shotgun, headed into town.

The McQueens were sitting on their front porch when she drove past. One stood up to get a better look at her car. They all watched her go by with dark expressions and without waving. That was okay, she didn't wave either.

Shortly after she passed the Dog Woods sign, she found the accident Colton from Fish and Game had warned her about. A utility truck from Montgomery Municipal was parked in front of the fallen pole with a few orange cones marking off the area. A new hole had been dug and a fresh pole planted to replace the one snapped off at about ground level. Currently, the long arm of the bucket truck was extended high in the air so two men, working side by side, could run new wires. Maybe she'd have power again by the time she got home. Karly was hopeful, though she still planned to pick up candles just in case.

It was a nice day, not too warm. Karly found a shady spot in front of the grocery store to park and before she went inside, she rolled the front windows down for Puppy's comfort.

She got a few staple items, cereal and milk, sandwich and salad fixings, and then spent several minutes wandering up and down the pet aisle, agonizing over dog food selections. Was Puppy an Iams dog? And, good night, how could this stuff be so expensive? She hadn't brought enough cash with her, not even to get a small bag. She ended up settling for Kibbles and Bits. Beefy bits, no less. With vegetables and real meat flavor, and supposedly all the nutrition that healthy, active dogs required. She picked up a collar too. If wandering free every morning became a habit, at least Puppy wouldn't be mistaken for a stray.

That he might already belong to someone else did cross Karly's mind. One didn't have to be wise in all things 'dog' to see he wasn't starving and his coat was well cared for. But if he did have another owner, then why didn't he go home when he had the chance? No, he'd come back to her instead. As far as Karly was concerned, unless she saw a crying child hanging 'Lost Dog' notices on the bullet-ridden Dog Woods sign, then Puppy's official home was now with her. She might not know anything about dogs, but she knew she wanted to keep him. He made her feel safe. He made her feel not quite so alone.

As she stood watching the cashier ring up her purchases, Karly considered all the things a newly-appointed pet owner probably ought to do. Like, take him to a vet, get him his shots, pick up some Frontline, and maybe get him neutered if he wasn't already. But on the tail end of that thought came the worry: Could Dan find her through vet records? Would she have to give her real name? Would she have to tell them where she lived? Her chest tightened, making it hard to breathe. Puppy wasn't scratching. Maybe this wasn't a high flea and tick area. And obviously he was healthy, despite his run-in with her front bumper. She paid for her groceries, already knowing there would be no vet. Not even for Puppy's well-being.

She was an awful person and a horrible pet owner, but she just couldn't risk it.

"Do you want some help out?" the cashier asked.

"No, thanks." Karly shouldered the bag of dog food and took what few sacks her meager groceries occupied. Two steps outside the store, however, she spotted a man standing at her car and froze.

Fish and Game; she recognized his uniform. Swallowing panic, Karly nearly ducked back into the store. Though his back was to her, she recognized Gabe almost instantly, but where was the sharp-eyed and deceptively easy-going Colton?

Hugging her groceries, Karly watched him warily. He was standing at her open passenger window, talking out loud to himself. No, he had to be on his radio, calling her car in. Karly's heart slammed inside her chest until she realized again, no, his radio was still clipped to his shirt and his hands were on his hips. If anything, he was talking to Puppy. Which was ridiculous. Almost as ridiculous as her trying to hide between the cart return and the gumball and sticker machines.

If he saw her like this, he would definitely get suspicious.

Karly made herself take several deep breaths. There was no place on this planet that she could hide where she would not encounter law enforcement of some kind. Just because Colton and this man, Gabe, were figures of constabulary authority, that did not automatically mean they talked to Dan. So long as she didn't do something to arouse their suspicions—actively behaving as if she wanted to avoid them, for instance—they would have no reason to go digging into who she really was.

Swallowing her tightly-rattled nerves and hugging her groceries, she headed for her car. As she drew steadily closer, Gabe suddenly threw back his head and barked with laughter. "Lap dog is a really good look for you."

"Shut up. Go away."

That was Colton. She'd recognize that deceptively honeyed tone anywhere, but where was he? Karly froze all over again. She ducked down, trying to see if there was another pair of boots on the far side of her car. But if Colton was on the driver's side, she couldn't see any sign of him. She crept closer, eyeing Gabe suspiciously.

Shaking his head, amusement heavy in his tone, Gabe asked, "What are you trying to do?"

"I'm sitting and I'm staying," the voice she could have sworn was Colton's dryly replied.

Gabe leaned over the window, resting his arm across the top of her car. "Buddy, she's got one hell of a surprise coming when she asks you to speak."

She was almost on them when she must have made a sound. Snapping upright, Gabe turned around and in the front seat of the car, a very human-looking shadow of a head ducked down out of sight. The car bounced. Karly almost dropped her groceries.

"Where's my dog?" she demanded, running the rest of the way while Gabe snatched his arm off the roof and quickly backed away. "What did you do with—" Ducking around the trunk, trying to keep the car between herself and Gabe, Karly froze when Puppy's massive furry head popped back up above the headrests. He looked at her, ears perked forward, tongue lolling.

Just Puppy. Not a man, like she had first believed. She blinked, confused. She could have sworn she'd seen…Heaven help her, but even knowing she'd find it empty, she still checked the backseat.

"Problem?" Gabe asked, pasting on a greeting smile.

"N-no." She didn't understand it, but Colton was nowhere in sight. Gabe had to have been on his radio after all. There was simply no other explanation.

She looked at him even more warily than before.

"Here," Gabe said, skirting around the back of the car to come and help her with the dog food. "Let me get that for you."

"I've got it." She ducked his outstretched hands and quickly wrenched open the back door to put her groceries on the seat.

Gabe slipped his hands into his back pockets and tried to affect a more harmless demeanor. "Nice looking dog you've got."

The knots in her stomach tightened. "Thanks." Realizing he might know Puppy wasn't hers and not wanting anyone to think she'd stolen him, she added, "Is he yours?"

"No, ma'am. These old woods are full of strays. What surprises me is how a wild boy like this would let you handle him."

"Puppy's very sweet," she said defensively.

From the passenger seat, Puppy groaned. Arching both eyebrows, Gabe suddenly tossed back his head with another barking laugh. "Puppy? You named him Puppy?"

Wondering why she was being singled out, even more defensively, Karly asked, "What's so funny?"

A low, ominous growl rumbled from the car, and Gabe responded instantly, raising his hands in placating surrender. He also dropped his laughing brown gaze and backed from the car.

"Not a thing, ma'am," he said, trying to get his mirth under control. "I just would have thought a big boy like this would be more of a Capone or a Cujo, or something. But big boys can be puppies too, can't they? Especially where pretty women are involved."

Uncomfortable, Karly shut the back of the car and approached the driver's door instead. Not wanting to look like she was running, she didn't get in right away. "Am I in violation of something?"

A flicker of surprise moved over Gabe's face. He looked at the car, his smile softening slightly before he added, "Not that I'm aware of. I'm just being friendly, that's all."

Karly wasn't ready for friendly. Not from strange men, and definitely not from strange policemen. "Then I can go?"

"Sure." Gabe took another backwards step, easing away from her car as if giving her plenty of room to flee.

Not that she was fleeing, Karly told herself. She was just going home.

"You take care," Gabe said as she got in behind the wheel. She clutched it with both hands so he would not see how badly she was shaking when he bent down, giving her another of his unassuming smiles through the driver's window. "Mama Margo said to tell you hello."

She didn't look at him. She was being rude and she knew it, but Karly was nervous and she couldn't help herself. She couldn't even make herself tell him to bid Margo thank you for the basket and that would have been completely normal. But no, she shoved the key in the ignition instead and quickly rolled up all the windows. She drove away slowly, but she probably looked like she was running anyway. Gabe watched her until she lost track of him in the rearview mirror. She was back on Old Bueller and halfway home before she remembered the newspaper she forgot to pick up.

"Damn it!"

She thought about going back to town, but she didn't think she could handle another run in with either Colton or Gabe. It was likely neither meant her any harm. Margo knew them and she didn't think Margo would send people who would hurt her to bring her sandwiches or to keep checking on her, but her hands wouldn't stop shaking. Her stomach felt so tangled and tight, she thought she might actually throw up, and when her cellphone rang, the sharp tones startled her so badly that she jumped half out of her skin.

"I forgot the newspaper," she said, without bothering to check the number. "What should I do? Should I go back and get one? I'm so scared, Beth. The local cops keep talking to me and—"

"You're fucked," Dan growled into her ear, his voice as cold and as sharp as knives.

Karly's throat seized so hard she choked. The next thing she knew, the car was fishtailing to a stop in the middle of the narrow dirt road. Without realizing it, she had slammed the brake pedal all the way down to the floor mat.

She sat behind the steering wheel, shaking hard, staring straight ahead without seeing anything.

"You want to run from me, baby? Fine, but there's no place in the world you can hide that I won't find you. You think you're scared now? Wait until we're face-to-face. Serve me fucking divorce papers? No, ma'am. 'Til death do us part. That's what you promised, and that's what I'll have. In every nuance and meaning of the word now, you…are…fucked."

Karly didn't have to hang up. The connection went dead in her trembling hand.

Seconds bled into minutes.

She couldn't move. She couldn't see. She couldn't even breathe.

She vaguely heard Puppy growl a half second before two hard knuckles tapped the glass right by her head.

Karly knew she was freaking out even while she did it, screaming and grabbing at the steering wheel. She even dropped her phone. If it weren't for the seatbelt, she'd have thrown herself into the passenger seat on top of Puppy, grabbing at him for security. Her eyes as huge as dinner plates, she stared at the very powerfully built man bending down to peer in through the window at her. His dark hair was shoulder length; his mustache, neatly trimmed. Tattoos wound up his arm all the way into his short sleeves. His hands were dirty, stained with engine oil. So was his bright orange t-shirt, which sported twin rifles crisscrossing one another and black, jagged letters that read, 'If you can read this, you're in range.'

He was a McQueen. He had to be. Her heart beat so hard, it hurt her ribs and still, when he tapped the window again and pointed groundward, she obeyed him, rolling the glass down just a crack.

Leaning his forearm along the roof of her car, McQueen looked at her. He looked at Puppy, dipped his head slightly to spit on the ground, and then looked back at her again when Puppy rumbled out another rolling growl.

"You lost?" he asked.

Karly shivered. Her wild glance darted from him to the dilapidated shacks sitting back from the road, nestled in amongst the shade trees. Two other men were sitting together on the front porch; another leaned against a support post with the long barrel of a rifle slung across his shoulders. Oh God, of all places to stop, she had stopped in front of their house.

Karly quickly shook her head. "No."

"You're the one moved into Margo's up the road, that right?"

Puppy bristled, loosing another low growl.

McQueen looked at him, unfazed. "I heard you, and I'm not talking to you." He stared at Karly again, then patted the top of her car twice. "Get on then." He gave a jerk of his head. "My driveway's not your parking lot."

Karly didn't need to be told twice. He was letting her go and she went, fairly flying the rest of the way home, driving much faster than she should have, much faster than was safe. She managed to stave off tears right up until her small cabin came into view, and then she lost it.

She couldn't remember turning the car off and she didn't get out. She just sat there, bawling and clinging first to the steering wheel and then to Puppy, who nosed his way into her arms and then sat stiff and still in the passenger seat while she leaned into him and gripped him like he was her lifeline. Her tears soaked his fur. Her panicked fingers pulled at his hair. But through it all, he made no move to break away and stayed with her until the storm of panic had subsided and the well of her tears ran dry. Her ragged breaths evened. She came back to herself enough to feel stupid and foolish.

"Sorry," she whispered, feeling even more foolish for apologizing to a dog, who couldn't understand her anyway.

As she pushed away from him, Puppy leaned over and nuzzled her cheek. The warm rasp of his tongue washed away a lingering tear. He offered no censure. He simply got out of the car when she did and followed her back into the house.

CHAPTER FIVE

Karly had lost her cellphone. How she could live in a cabin this small with so few belongings, and still lose something as vital as her phone?

She remembered snapping two quick pictures of her black eye and sending them to her lawyer. She thought she remembered plugging it into its charger on the kitchen counter afterward, but a few hours later as she came to the fridge to grab a quick bite for lunch, she noticed it wasn't there. Turning in a slow circle, she eyed the counter, the bar that separated the tiny kitchen from the equally tiny living room, and the table. She searched the floor the same way. She even got down on her hands and knees and looked under first the stove and then the fridge.

Karly tore the house apart, searching everywhere—under the front porch, under the bed, in the yard. Though she hadn't gone anywhere since she'd used it, she even searched her car, but the phone was gone.

She began to panic. How could she have lost it like this unless someone had…had what? Snuck into her house and swiped it, with all the doors and windows locked and both her and Puppy never hearing a sound? That was paranoia, pure and simple. The phone was here. Somewhere. It just had to be.

She got out of the car, slamming the door behind her, and ran back into the cabin. She tore through it all over again—ripping the sheets off the bed and shaking them out, sticking her hand down the into the toilet pipe, dragging everything out from under both the kitchen and the bathroom sinks—only to find her phone midway into a full-blown panic attack, stuck between the sofa cushions, exactly where she knew she'd already searched at least twice before. How could she have missed it? Dropping to the floor with relief, she hugged it to her chest as if she were drowning and it were her only lifeline.

The heat of a warm body sat down beside her. She wrapped her arms around him and buried her face in his fur. She felt so foolish. "I'm such an idiot."

He took her hug stoically, but she felt it when his head turned, ears swiveling toward the door. Then she heard it too, footsteps crunching up the gravel walk toward her front porch.

Everything inside of her froze. That same icy panic that had seized her back when she thought her phone had been taken swelled inside her a hundred times stronger than it had before and every bit as irrational. She should have left Dan years ago. She never should have married him at all. She hated this frightened rabbit of a person that she had become because of him.

"Hello, the house!" a woman called, her thumping footsteps already climbing the porch steps. She was halfway to the door before Karly recognized the voice. Not Dan; not Colton; not some stranger. Just Mama Margo, the very nice old woman who had sent her a food basket because the power was out and she was new.

Karly pushed up off the floor and went to meet her. "Afternoon." She pushed open the door to allow the old woman inside. "Where's your car? You didn't walk here all the way from town, did you?"

"Walking's good for you." Stopping just over the threshold, Margo locked eyes with Puppy and frowned, her fists knuckling into her hips. Her frown deepened and her eyes narrowed the longer Puppy pretended not to notice her standing there, then she looked at Karly. "What have you done to yourself? You look awful."

"Thanks," Karly dead-panned. "You should have seen me this morning. Did you come for your basket?"

The old woman made a rude sound, waving that off with a careless hand. "Keep it. I've got hundreds of the damn things—every Mother's Day, just like clockwork, I'm inundated: chocolates, fruit, sausage and cheese, with those fancy-ass little cracker things. What the hell's wrong with Triscuits, I ask you? Tried and true, my girl, stick with what works and leave the fancy-ass things alone." Drawing her diminutive frame upright, she knuckled her fists into her plump hips and glared at Karly. "I need a ride."

Now Puppy looked at her.

So did Karly. She opened her mouth, only just catching herself before her question regarding the benefits of walking could be mistaken for sarcasm. "Uh, okay." Giving herself a slight shake, she turned to get her purse. "Where do you want to go?"

"North Ridge," Margo said. "It's the Hunt Festival this week. Whole town's attending. And you did not just growl at me, you arrogant, insolent pup!" she snapped, turning to glare directly at Puppy. That Karly became instantly alarmed was no small thing. Neither was Puppy's abrupt silence. He froze where he was. His big wolfish body didn't exactly drop into a submitting posture, but it did droop, his head lowering, his tail...not quite tucking, but definitely down. Karly tried to step in between Margo and Puppy, but the old woman leaned around her and continued to berate the now tense and silent dog. "We've got folks coming in from as far away as Texas and even Colorado. We have an *obligation* to put in an appearance, whether we want to or not!"

"Why are you yelling at my dog?" Karly stared at her. If she weren't seeing this now with her own eyes, she never would have guessed her to be this insane.

"Because we've got responsibilities! We're *hosting*!" Margo stopped yelling at Puppy and turned back to her. "The guests began arriving and no one was there to greet them. Get your coat. Looks like rain."

"You want me to greet your guests." Pulling back, Karly shook her head. "I-I've got no problem driving you, Margo, but I'm a guest here myself. I don't think I should—"

"You live here now, that means you represent us and have every bit as much a right to attend the town festivals as anyone else. Besides, folks won't cotton to people they don't see." The old woman headed back down off the porch. "Put your sunglasses on. No one will notice your eye."

The bruise was larger than the lens on her sunglasses so Karly knew that was a lie. But for all that she wanted to keep arguing, in the end, she dug her glasses out of her purse and reluctantly put them on. She also dug out her keys and, bracing herself to endure a long afternoon of being stared at and whispered about, she patted her leg. "Come on, Puppy."

"Leave him," Margo said gruffly. "He can't do his job and shadow you too." Having just reached the passenger side of Karly's car, the old woman turned and pointed back, not at Karly, but at the rather-chastened massive black dog who had followed only as far as the front door. "Whatever he has to, that's what Alphas do—they get the job done regardless of personal feelings! You stepped into that job, my boy. No one forced you. So shape up!"

Mama Margo either wasn't in her right mind or she wasn't a dog person, Karly couldn't tell which. But those concerns must have shown on her face because, glancing up from Puppy to her, Mama Margo rolled her eyes. She rolled her hand too, gesturing in the general direction of the cabin. "And, of course, they...protect the house...or something."

Karly shut Puppy inside the cabin. She eyed the old woman cautiously, following her out to her car despite the scratch and whine she heard at the door. Glimpsing movement at the window curtains, she glanced back just as Puppy jumped onto the back of the couch, nosing the curtains apart to watch her go. He put one paw on the glass, as if in farewell.

She waved back, wishing she could bring him along. She would have felt safer with him along (how silly, she thought, it's not like you're going into a war zone), but neither did she want to agitate Mama Margo further.

"Day's wasting," Margo called.

Folks won't cotton to someone they don't see.

Karly didn't think she needed the people of Hollow Hills to "cotton" to her, but neither did she want to be ostracized by an entire town. Not even a small one, especially since she didn't know how long she was going to have to hide here. Still, she wasn't looking forward to spending the afternoon as the focus of a lot of whispering and gossip. Just the idea of it made her stomach twist so hard she thought she might be sick.

"Don't you let him win, girl," Mama Margo growled, her weathered face as hard as time and hard-scrabble living could make a woman. The old woman looked pointedly at her eye. "Don't you dare. He might have taken a woman and turned her into a rabbit, but you've still got a choice: Hide here in your warren, or grow your gumption back and fight on."

Her keys were cutting into her palm, Karly squeezed them so hard. "I don't think I have any gumption anymore."

A touch of sympathy flittered through Mama Margo's dark eyes and then was gone again. She came back to Karly. "Of course you do. I'll bet you can even feel it if you try. It's right here—" She lay her hand over Karly's stomach and held it there, as if waiting for the moth-fluttering movement of an unborn child. "—burning and churning inside you, eager to get out again. And it's here, too." She tapped two wrinkled, arthritic fingers to Karly's chest, and then again, higher up at her temple. "And here. I've eaten enough rabbit in my life to know it when I see one." Backing up a step, the old woman shook both her head and her finger. "You…you're no rabbit, in spite of what he's done. And call me Mama Margo. Everybody does."

Karly stood captured in her unblinking stare until, wisdom imparted, Mama Margo gave a satisfied nod and returned to stand by the car. With one hand on the handle, she stared out over the roof and waited to be let in.

The keys trembling in her hand, wondering why Mama Margo's odd assurance should leave her feeling so…relieved, Karly unlocked the passenger door first before heading around to the other side of the car.

"Don't worry," Mama Margo said with a sniff. "I've already told everyone to expect you. Even the out-of-towners will behave themselves."

Karly glanced longingly back at the cabin, but she couldn't see Puppy in the window any more. Her shoulders drooped. She really wished he were coming with her. Biting back a sigh, she unlocked the car and got in behind the wheel.

* * * * *

The minute Karly's car left the driveway, disappearing down the road behind a curtain of old oaks and towering evergreens, Colton had the back door open and was running just as fast as he could for North Ridge. He pushed hard, leaping over runnels and rocks, ascending the steep hills toward the Hunt grounds. The wolf in him reveled in the run, in the wind that whipped his fur and the heavy forest smells that assaulted his senses. The exertion felt good, though he pushed—faster and faster—until it became a punishing hurt. The shadow-cooled dirt under his paws felt good. Doing what he knew he had to, even that felt good in an odd way, though he knew this could very well end up being the worst mistake of his own, personal life.

Alphas didn't have personal lives. Alphas lived for the good of the pack, the good of his people and his town. Mama Margo was right. He had responsibilities that could not be pushed aside, not for anyone. Not even for Karly. He wished he knew what it was about her that pulled at him so strongly. All he did know, was that he felt *something*…a connection, maybe…between them. It gnawed at him every time he looked at that bruise on her face, every time a strange sound made her jump, every time she clutched at him for strength while she trembled from a lack of it.

Who had been on the other end of that phone call? He'd taken her phone wanting to find out, but he hadn't anticipated how quickly she'd notice it missing or how frantic she'd become trying to find it again. Fortunately, the call that had distressed her had been the last received. He'd had to memorize the number, but as soon as he could, he was going to run it. Then he'd know exactly who, where and what she was so afraid of.

Colton ran harder, faster, hoping Mama Margo had the sense to let Karly drive her up the scenic route. He had to get to the North Ridge first. Again, he didn't know why. It was instinctive, a driving need to disassociate himself from "Puppy" and see her with his human eyes, to speak and interact with her on two legs instead of four.

What would she do, he wondered, when there was no door for her to hold between them?

He burst from the woods into a clearing filled with cars and trucks of every imaginable make, model and color. They were parked in tight and close in order to accommodate as many as possible, but a long line of cars still extended down the winding road that led from the interstate to the North Ridge parking lot. Glinting metal and windshields shone in the sunlight, lining the blacktop as far as he could see before the trees swallowed them from sight.

The smell of excitement was everywhere. Brightly colored pennants snapped in the breeze, signaling which roped off areas were for what game. Men were grunting and shouting, women were calling and laughing, pups were squealing in play, some were crying—the mated females and elderly would be tending them and he knew they had a long list of activities planned to keep the little ones both entertained and safe.

Colton stopped in the midst of that ocean of vehicles, tail and ears both up, listening, quivering, letting the excitement wash over him before he began to wind his way through the parking lot. He found his truck parked under the partial shade of a flowering dogwood. Gabe was there, sitting in the back of the truck, checking his watch and sipping on a Coke. He straightened when he noticed Colton wending through the densely parked cars, and set his drink aside. Hopping down to fish the truck keys out of his pocket, he did a startled double-take just as Colton began to change—arching as he shifted, the sting of metamorphosis heightening the near sensual sensation of lupine lines growing, rippling and stretching into the bigger, heavier form of a man.

It wasn't until he felt the sudden constriction that he remembered Karly's collar.

Crap.

He jerked up from four legs onto two and just as the final part of the shift rippled out through his paws, stretching them into useful hands once more, he grabbed for the collar and quickly took it off. Too late. Gabe was already laughing.

"Does she take you for your evening walk, too?" he asked as he opened the driver's door and then stepped out of the way. "Down to the corner oak until you do your business and then back home again?"

Colton gave him a dirty look and threw the collar in the truck. Thank God for bachelors. His clothes were still wadded up behind the seat. He grabbed his pants. "I want you to run a trace on a phone number."

Snorting, still amused, Gabe half-shrugged. "Sure."

"How's the wind blowing?"

"Pretty quiet, really." He glanced back across the parking lot to watch three young women, talking and laughing as they made their way toward the snapping pennants. Pacing down the length of the truck, Gabe scented after them, but stopped at the tailgate. "Nice," he commented, before giving himself a slight shake and coming back to Colton. "There've been a few fights, but nothing unexpected. Jax is here. Brought a whole posse of his boys down to get their Brides— eleven. Ha! Eleven! All in one year? Yeah, they're definitely looking to break out from under Daddy Deacon's restraining arm and expand into a territory of their own. Nobody likes the way they keep saying how 'peaceful' it is here."

"Jax is barely weaned," Colton grunted, jerking his pants up over his lean hips. "If he starts sniffing out of line, I'll take him to the woodshed and he's just smart enough to know it. I'm not worried about Jax." His father, the Alpha Deacon, was something else entirely though. "What else?"

"Nothing much. Ben Fortimer threatened to plant a load of buckshot in little Jimmy Bingham's tail if he comes sniffing around his daughter one more time. She entered herself in the Hunt, but I don't think daddy's quite ready to see his baby girl tackled to the forest floor. Pain in the ass stuff; nothing we can't handle. Now, since I'm not going to be distracted from this, let's talk about you some more."

Buttoning and zipping up, Colton gave him a hard glare.

"Tell me," Gabe said, cheerfully ignoring it. "What sort of fool collars a wolf?"

Off the top of his head, Colton was inclined to think one who didn't know any better. He draped his shirt over his shoulder, but didn't bother putting it on. Few of this year's bachelor males had. When one only had four days to impress a wolf-shifting female into letting herself be caught without getting one's face bitten off, one started by showing off his physique and it helped if it was exceptional. Colton was fortunate to be blessed in that regard.

"People are starting to say things," Gabe offered, seeming so casual and yet definitely not.

Putting on his socks and boots, Colton frowned. "Like what?" He was pretty sure he already knew.

"Like who is that beat-up blonde and is the Hollow Hills' Alpha really mating her or just being protective?"

Colton glared at him for almost a full minute before yanking his laces tight, grabbing the truck door and slamming it somewhat harder than was required. "Let's go find our Brides," he growled, and headed for the gaming ground.

CHAPTER SIX

There were potential Brides everywhere and they were, all of them, in his nose, and yet Colton knew it almost from the second that Karly stepped from her car onto Hollow Hills' traditional Hunting grounds. Not only did every sentry chuff and rumble an under-breath alert to let everyone else know they'd been invaded, but the wind picked just that moment to kick up and shift and suddenly, her scent was all that he could smell. It stiffened him. In more ways than one, damn it. There were too many females here and every nerve in him was primed to take one—which only made Karly's pleasing scent that much harder to resist. It was the impending Hunt. The wolf in him was right beneath the surface of his skin, begging to be loosed. Even knowing he shouldn't, he still turned to follow that whisper-soft breath of Karly, his predator eyes hunting the crowd until he saw her walking with Mama Margo, there among the tents and vendors.

In the next instant, a football smacked into his chest and bounced right off him. The next thing Colton knew, fifteen shirtless males, all of them as driven to impress as he was, pile-slammed him to the ground.

Young Jax Deacon landed directly on top of him, pant-laughing at him. He was a kid, barely twenty and still with that wiry, puppy-lean physique that hadn't yet filled out into manhood. Any other year, Colton would have let his wolf out. Any other year, it would have been expected. But then, any other year there wouldn't have been a human wandering among the mating games.

Growling, Colton waited for the pile to gradually untangle itself and, when Jax seemed content to take his own, sweet time getting up, Colton "helped" the whelp. His shove almost threw the boy, but Jax landed with awkward grace on his feet and, as they stalked away from one another, grinned back at Colton.

The wolf in him—teased by scents of so many tantalizing females, the proximity of a good mating run, and the instinctive agitation amplified by so many trespassing males—leapt to answer that grin like the challenge it was surely meant to be. Colton barely kept his temper

"Hey!" Colton turned to see Gabe waiting for him near another shirtless male, an Omega named Marcus. Scarred and tattooed, he'd come to the Ridge dressed in biker leathers, on the back of a Harley and looking for a pack to join. Colton had no idea why he hadn't approached a stronger Alpha like Deacon.

"Can you give me loyalty?" Colton had asked the first time he'd met him.

"Can you earn it?" had been Marcus's reply.

Yeah, Colton had pretty much liked him right from the start. He didn't trust him yet, but he liked him.

Shaking his head, Gabe spread his arms as if to say, 'I tossed you the ball, man. What the hell?'

Snorting to clear Karly's distracting scent out of his nose, Colton stalked through the grass to join them. He had to pay better attention than this or he wasn't going to impress anyone, and he knew it. Dropping into a tackling position, he glared straight across fifteen or so feet of open grass and dirt to where his immediate opponent crouched in anticipation of meeting his charge.

To any outsider, this might look like a ragtag game of touch football, skins versus skins with no clear-cut team lines drawn, but it wasn't. There were nine packs in the Hunt this year. Nine. If that wasn't a record, Colton couldn't remember any year that beat it. They might square off as if there were two opposing sides, but in this game, it was every male for himself, with pack brothers loosely joined together in an effort to monopolize the ball. It was all about proving oneself the fittest, the strongest, the most aggressive, dangerous. And virile. Females lined the ropes, watching, sometimes cheering, mostly just picking out who they might like to run for later on. As the hosting Alpha, Colton knew more than a few were looking at him, but as he settled into the next line-up and hunkered down into position behind the quarterback, his eyes searched for only one person: Karly. She hadn't even noticed he was here yet.

"Hup!"

The ball shunted right. Only half the players chased it; the other half went straight for targeted competitors. Colton went straight for Jax. One of his pack brothers tried to run interference, but too late, Jax realized his intent and he took the young boy down. It was a hard landing, one made infinitely harder when Colton rolled to slam him facedown into the dirt and pin him there.

"Be careful," he growled into the young whelp's ear. He didn't need to say anything more. Shoving back to his feet, he let the boy go.

Jax rose to his knees slowly, a scrape on his chin and blood pouring from his nose. Raw fury lit his eyes; they were so yellow, Colton barely suppressed his own inner wolf's answering surge.

"Be very careful," Colton warned again, and then he turned to walk away.

Gabe's shout a half second later sounded tinny, like the echo of a cry at the very end of a long tunnel, and Colton didn't need it to know he was being attacked. He felt it, that electrified prickle of all the tiny hairs rising on the back of his neck a half second before the hard pound of Jax's feet charged the ground directly behind him. His instinctive response was all savage—a hard duck right, pivot and grab. Hands locked on Jax's throat and then his groin. Colton heaved, flinging the reckless youth up into the air before slamming him down again, flat on his back in the grass and dirt, faster than the boy's expression could even register the failure and then the subsequent pain.

Colton pinned him by his throat this time, pressing the force of his defeat and the pain into every inch of Jax's wiry frame, looming so close over him that all Colton could see was his own reflection and the flicker of fear that flitted through the younger man's eyes.

"When you find your balls," he growled, "come and challenge me again. But next time, do it right. Come at my back again and, Deacon's pup or not, I'll kill you."

In a move so slight, Colton doubted anyone else might even see it, Jax lifted his chin. A symbolic flash of throat, an act of placating submission that was neither honest nor reached as far as the younger *volka's* eyes.

Colton stood up slowly, giving Jax plenty of time to decide if he wanted to lash out now or later. Jax didn't move. He waited until Colton was far enough away before sitting up, then wiped his bloody nose on his arm.

Later it was.

Turning away, Colton stopped when he saw Karly and Mama Margo, standing side-by-side at the pennant-dotted rope that walled off the field. They were staring straight at him. Karly's eyes were huge and she'd covered her mouth. Why couldn't she have spotted him while he was strutting his stuff, running the ball down the field, naked from the waist up, a strong male in his absolute prime…no. She had to wait until he was beating up a stupid kid—*that* she saw.

Crap.

Mama Margo nodded once, approval shining in the depths of those calculating eyes; Karly, on the other hand, looked appalled.

She also looked really pretty. The wind was tugging at her hair. The sun had ignited all those golden strands, turning them into a soft halo of light all around her head and shoulders. The urge to go and talk to her was powerful, but right then, Gabe passed into Colton's field of vision, with Marcus not far behind and watching closely.

Gabe threw his arms out, an exaggerated shrug coupled with a look that said plainly, *Seriously, what the hell are you doing?*

Colton didn't know anymore. He looked back at Karly, but her attention had been diverted. Sebastian McQueen was talking to her now, his posture looming and possessive. A shot of red burned straight up his spine and embedded itself under the back of Colton's skull. For several long seconds, it turned everything he could see a dark and throbbing shade of rage. He gripped his fists so tightly his knuckles popped, and before he knew it, he was stalking toward them.

"Hey!" Gabe was already walking backwards to join the next line up, but his look said everything.

And he was right, Colton had to stop this. He had to get his mind on the game. He had to—

Karly reached out and let McQueen's larger, more powerful hand engulf her own.

He had to kill that motherfucker right there where he stood.

Colton almost lost it. He nearly shifted. He nearly charged with all the force and aggression that could be packed into his powerful frame, straight for McQueen's throat. He nearly did a lot of things, but in the end, he kept control. Colton snapped around to rejoin Gabe and Marcus in the next line-up.

"Who's the woman?" Marcus asked. "And is she going to be a problem?"

"Get your nose off her before I slap it," Colton said testily. He was angry and itching in his own skin—it felt so restricting.

Marcus pant-laughed, but when Colton hunkered down to square off against the opposing team, both Marcus and Gabe hunkered down at his flanks.

Colton tried to keep his burning eyes on his next opponent—a large male, shirtless, one of Jax's lieutenants and old enough to want to play at being a man, though still too young to be any kind of threat in a real Hunt. Colton took his measure and then his attention was locked on McQueen once more.

He meant to play the game. He truly did, but there was a fizzling sensation trickling up his spine and into the back of his head, prickling like needles to get in under the haze of red creeping in around him. He'd never felt his rising wolf quite like this before; Colton struggled to swallow it back.

Karly's hand was still in McQueen's. She didn't seem in that big of a hurry to retract it.

"Hup!"

The ball was spiked and two rows of aggressive wolf-shifters in full-on mate-mode surged toward one another. With his very first step, Colton felt the subdermal rip that tore him from the last vestiges of his shredded civility. The gloves came off; up until that moment, he hadn't realized he'd been wearing any.

Jax's lieutenant hit him like a brick wall, but Colton was older, bigger, and pissed off. One hard right hook knocked the youth flat on his back with a dislocated jaw and at least one less tooth. What was it about twenty-something pups that made them think they were wolf enough to compete with the big boys? When Colton had done the same some ten years ago, the lesson had cost him a savage mauling and a broken leg. Jax's lieutenant only paid with a dislocated knee, a few facial injuries, and a breath-robbing body slam to the ground. He would not be running for a Bride this year, but at least he could count himself damned lucky there was a human on the field, otherwise Colton would have let his wolf out.

Of course, if not for Karly, Colton wouldn't be the only wolf and this would have been a much more savage game. The shine of lupine eyes all over the field told of more than one *volka* on the brink of losing his restraint.

Leaving the whelp rolling on the ground, clutching his leg and grunting cries of pain, Colton headed back to wait for the next line-up and let Jax and his pack mates help their wounded brother to the sidelines. He couldn't help himself, he glanced back over his shoulder. Sebastian McQueen had drawn Karly away from the game and, with Mama Margo quietly chaperoning in their shadow, he was leading her deeper into the crowd. Away from Colton.

Where anything could happen.

The whole field flashed an even darker shade of red. Colton didn't realize he was growling until he began to catch looks from other males nearby. The level of aggression spiked all around him. Everywhere that he could see, yellow ferocity was igniting in the depths of warrior eyes. A wave of echoing growls rippled through the field as the wolf rose perilously close to the surface of those around him.

The next line-up began to organize. Colton hunkered into position, muscles tense—he should go after Karly, get her away from McQueen before the sonofabitch did something he'd have to kill him for. His *volka* rage was not yet so blinding that he failed to notice all of Jax's remaining lieutenants lining up opposite of him. Seeking revenge for their fallen brother, their eyes were bright and some of them were snarling through bared teeth.

The aggression inside him grew cold and sprouted fangs.

Bring it.

Dual growls sounded from both sides of him as Gabe and Marcus both took up defensive positions at his flanks. Marcus flexed, ready and willing to take this hit for an Alpha he barely knew. Gabe, Colton knew, would probably chew his ears about this for days to come, but in this instance, they were at his side, offering pack strength and support.

"Hup!"

Colton was still a bulldozer, only now there were a hell of a lot more walls. They took his ass straight to the ground, and in the fury and pain that followed as teeth fastened onto his arm, and as fists and feet began to pummel his gut, the wolf in him broke free.

* * * * *

"Don't be afraid," McQueen said, showing her the gun.

"I'm not afraid." But Karly was shaking so badly, she knew he had to know that was a lie.

Her next door neighbor, a man who looked every bit as hard and rough as the surrounding mountains, remained gentle and calm. He extended his hand, as steady as stone. "It's not going to bite you. Here, take it."

Karly glanced sideways, throwing a 'save me' look to Mama Margo, but she had been waylaid some time ago by a pack of squealing, happy children. A wilder bunch, Karly had never encountered in her life. That the morning had been spent running through the woods was obvious. They were dirty, sweaty, thrilled to be here, and the moment they'd seen Mama Margo, they had come running bearing gifts— flowers, rocks, a feather, a lizard's discarded tail (said lizard still being imprisoned deep in the coverall pocket of the boy who'd caught it), even a spider.

Mama Margo, bless her, studied each and every treasure brought to her with all the seriousness and pride that each child seemed to think it deserved. That left Karly feeling very much alone in this corner of the field, with Sebastian McQueen standing between her and the rest of the festival taking place through the woods behind them.

"Take it," he said again, and Karly waffled, both wincing and tsking as she accepted the butt of the revolver.

She held it, pinched between two fingers. "Now what?"

McQueen snorted. "Not like that." His hand on hers was big and calloused, rough as sandpaper, but gentle in motion as he shifted her grip, forcing her palm to conform to the wood grip and really hold it. "Not too tight or too loose. Feel the weight."

It was heavier than it looked and, for some reason, his hands on hers made her nervous. She tried not to let it bother her, but her gaze kept shifting to Mama Margo, who never glanced her way long enough to notice.

55

"Put your finger on the trigger, but don't pull it. Just get comfortable with it and with the idea of pulling it." Sliding his arm around her waist, McQueen slipped into position behind her. His chest touched her back. It felt very hot and hard, very solid. "Don't worry," he rumbled, his low voice tickling at the nape of her neck. "This won't hurt a bit."

That made her even more nervous. Everything about him made her uncomfortable. She couldn't help looking around, but they were far enough from the main festival ground that all she could see were the distant tent tops and the snap of a few wind-blown pennants. She could hear the crowd, but it was doubtful if anyone there would hear her if she needed them to. Mama Margo and the kids were no help at all, and McQueen…he held her close, far too intimately for her liking, but there was no polite way to extract herself. When he tapped at her feet with his, she dutifully moved hers apart and took up a shooter's stance.

"Now, take a deep breath." His hands slid down her arms, coming to rest under her hands, and together, they raised the gun. "Relax. Don't lock your arms. That's the way. Line up the site with your target."

Straight ahead of them, Karly focused on the first of three partially squashed beer cans that had been set along the flat edge of an old tree trunk some fifty feet away.

"Deep breath," McQueen said. "When you're ready, don't pull the trigger; squeeze it. Soft and slow. Like you mean it."

The heat and the strength of him scared her. She was encircled by arms that felt like bands of warm steel. All she could think about was how much it would hurt to get hit by hands like his. All she wanted to do was run, but she just couldn't make herself move.

"Deep breath," he said again, and she shivered. "Don't be afraid. Squeeze the trigger."

Somewhere in the distance, perhaps even on Colton's savage football field, someone must have scored a goal because all of a sudden, she could hear shouting, cheering…and howling, of all things.

She started to look back, but McQueen's next rumbling murmur stopped everything.

"You feel good in my arms," he said.

She stiffened. If not for his hands, she would have dropped the gun; if not for his arms, she'd have twisted away and put immediate space between them. "Let go of me, please," she whispered, and oh how she hated herself for how badly her broken voice shook when she said it.

"Mm," he growled, a strangely seductive sound that rolled out of him and shivered into her. "Why else would you come to the Hunting ground, if not for this? You want to be bred."

"What?!" The word squeaked out of her.

He shifted his hand, abandoning hers to drop and settle his, like a burning brand, low on her abdomen. The internal havoc that caused was instantaneous. She flinched, every inch of her in immediate revolt as she jerked around to push him away. His arms tightened, startling her budding struggles into stillness the instant his mouth captured hers.

Karly hit him. She hadn't known she was going to until her fist was balled and—no maidenly slap, this—she swung. Every one of her knuckles cracked against his jaw. It worked, but only in the sense that she knocked his mouth off of hers.

McQueen laughed, licking at the hint of blood just beginning to well up at the corner of his mouth. "Spirited, too. I like that."

He took his gun away from her, then reached for her again, and suddenly they were both struck from the side by a massive, furry weight. Karly grabbed reflexively, catching fistfuls of black hair in both hands as all three of them went straight to the ground. She hit her knees, but it wasn't until she heard the first ferocious snarl that she realized what had knocked her over.

"Puppy!" she gasped. She didn't know how he'd managed to escape the house, but that he was here in defense of her was unmistakable. Although she had taken part of the impact, she was not the focus of the dog's attack. His hackles were up, every hair on his tense body was standing on end, and his teeth were bared in snarl after rasping snarl. He looked deadly as he crouched on top of Sebastian McQueen, every breath an exhaling growl of intense dislike.

McQueen lay exactly as he'd fallen, sprawled on his back with his hands up, neither defensively nor offensively poised. Not yet, anyway. His eyes, which she could have sworn mere seconds ago were dark brown, were now so brightly yellow that she wondered how she could ever have mistaken them for anything other than gold. All those bad jokes about redneck country and family inbreeding must hit close to the truth; everyone here had the strangest damn eyes!

"No! No, Puppy!" Scrambling to her knees, Karly grabbed for his scruff. He must have lost his collar when he had escaped the house because he wasn't wearing it now. That made holding him a heck of a lot harder. "Down. Get down!"

"You don't impress me, boy," McQueen told the dog. He laughed, a low, growling chuckle that somehow seemed to make his eyes shine even more yellow than before. "Puppy. How fitting."

The snarl that rolled out of Puppy then was unlike any sound she had ever heard an animal make before. He lunged and, if not for Karly's arms locked around his throat and chest, would have gone right for McQueen's throat.

"Run!" she told him, barely keeping her grip on the impossibly strong dog. That he didn't turn and bite at her in his fury to free himself was something she wouldn't think about for hours yet to come. She heaved and struggled, dragging Puppy back by mere inches, but McQueen only rolled and now he too was in a position to attack.

"I don't think so," he growled. "This has been a long time in coming, hasn't it…Puppy?" His smile was all teeth, and in that tense moment when the only thought she had, centered on whether or not she might have to save her dog from her neighbor, Karly suddenly realized they weren't alone any more. There were people standing like shadows in the field all around them. Silent as ghosts, they watched, as if the outcome of this grossly outmatched confrontation between man and beast were instead something of paramount importance. Worse yet, there were other dogs. Three huge and snarling grays—wolves, her brain tried to label them; but there was just no way that could be true—came out of the grass behind McQueen.

"Oh my God," Karly whispered, clinging to Puppy even tighter, scared to death that, if those dogs—wolves; no, no way—launched at her, she would let go and if she did, then all she could do was watch as her dog was torn to pieces right there in front of her.

"Help me!" she cried, and it wasn't until she twisted to beg those closest behind her for aid that she saw two more wolves—dogs; no, it was getting harder and harder to believe canines this huge could be anything as common as dogs—closing in directly behind them. She stiffened, panic rising like vomit in the back of her throat, but she was not their target. They drew in, a flank of support behind Puppy, hackles raised, sharp teeth bared in deadly serious intent although neither made a single sound beyond the billows-like rush of their indrawn breaths.

"Come to me, girl." Mama Margo came up through the tall grass directly behind them. She was the only one looking at Karly, her age-lined face a mask completely without compassion. "Let him go."

"No!" Karly gasped, her arms tightening protectively around Puppy's neck and chest. His whole body felt stiff and ready. Every breath he took was still a growl and he wasn't backing down.

"Things like this should be settled, not left to fester." Mama Margo held out her hand, beckoning. "Come. Let him go. The winner will be Alpha of us all."

Karly stared at her. Funny, how crazy often never showed on the surface. It took something like this for it to expose itself clearly.

Shaking her head, barely resisting the urge to shout at her adoptive town that they were, all of them, lunatics, Karly heaved at Puppy, shoving and muscling him back inch after too-small inch until, at last, he shuddered and abruptly relented. When he retreated, so did the wolves at his back; McQueen and his wolves followed with their eyes, but did not pursue them when she dragged Puppy back. She didn't want them to, but the two wolves that supported him followed her.

"Spirited. I like that." McQueen's smile became a smirk. "Come back and run with us, if you want to," he called after her. "I'll show you how an Alpha runs his bitch to ground."

Puppy tried to turn back, but Karly kept him moving. People were staring as she left. Some snorted, others shook their heads; why did it suddenly feel as if she'd made a shameful mistake? She couldn't understand it, but by the time she reached the parking lot, Puppy's head was down and his tail was practically tucked. Those two other wolves following a good thirty feet behind her, even they looked chastened. She didn't understand that either, but she kept a wary eye on them and her fingers locked in Puppy's fur until she got him safely locked inside her car.

Mama Margo hadn't followed them. Well, Mama Margo was going to have to find another ride home, because there was no way Karly was going to stay after this. Watching those stray wolves—she shivered—Karly climbed in behind the steering wheel and did not stop driving until she and Puppy were once again safely back home.

CHAPTER SEVEN

"His name is Dan Whitaker, and he's a cop out of Redemption," Gabe said, handing Colton the paper he'd brought to this clandestine meeting in the middle of the night. A chronic smiler under most circumstances, there were lines now around Gabe's eyes and mouth, and none of them had anything to do with amusement. "Read this. The BOLO came in while we were up on the Ridge."

Colton had to turn the fax sheet into the headlights of the truck. He didn't bother reading the description, but simply stared at Karly's black and white photo. Her last name was Whitaker, not Smith. That part wasn't surprising. It only made sense for a woman, scared and on the run, to want to change her name. But the other part, the married part...that did surprise him. No. No, surprise wasn't quite the right word for what he was feeling. Her husband—a cop no less—had put that bruise on her face.

The paper crinkled as his hands tightened on the edges. He had to force himself to relax before he ripped it the way he so badly wanted to rip into her husband for every moment of brutality the *chelovak* had visited upon his Karly.

His Karly?

She wasn't his, and the BOLO picture showed that. It was a wedding photograph. Karly looked beautiful, standing alone on the steps of a white church. She wasn't much younger than she was now and her eyes were so carefree and shining that he couldn't help but wonder if the day that picture was taken weren't the last time she'd been so happy...or bruise-free.

Gabe stood silently by, waiting while he looked his fill.

"What do you want me to do?" Gabe finally asked.

"Place a call to Jefferson in Grady. He might know someone over Redemption way. At the very least, he can cancel the BOLO without it leading back to us. This...Whitaker will have to do some fast talking if he tries to reinstate it. Something tells me, questions are the last thing that sonofabitch is going to want." Dan Whitaker wasn't in the photo. The picture had been carefully edited to leave nothing more than a disembodied hand upon her waist, but Colton stared at that, unblinking while the tick of his temper began to build behind his eyes.

"Some fellow came through town this afternoon," Gabe reluctantly volunteered. "I didn't see him, but Hays says he was asking after her."

Colton drew a deep breath, trying to control the protective wrath of the wolf within. "Somebody already knows she's here then. Who was he? Where is he now?"

"No idea on either count. He didn't stick around."

"Anybody talk to him?"

"And risk Mama Margo's temper? Not a chance."

Colton snorted, budding anger giving way to rueful laughter as he considered the old woman. "I've never seen her take to anyone so fast or so fondly." He looked at Karly's photo again, as if trying to memorize the soft lines of her unmarred face. "What about Marcus? Where is he?"

"Camping up on the Ridge last I saw."

"Who's he talking to?"

"No one that I've seen. He's been keeping his distance pretty much since he got here."

"Did you run his bike?"

"Yeah, he's got a couple misdemeanors and a few traffic violations. Nothing unforgiveable or more recent than nine years ago. He seems decent enough. Says he's not interested in a Bride, but he'll run interference for you until you get one."

Yeah, Colton liked him, all right. Usually, he was a pretty good judge of character. It was just that right now, when the very thought of Karly turned every other thought inside out in his head, Colton found himself uncertain which instincts to trust. "Are my clothes in the truck or are they still on the field?"

"I've got 'em tucked up under the seat. What's the plan?"

He had no clear idea. Folding the BOLO in half and then half again, Colton ran his thumbnail along the crease and glanced back up the road toward the cabin, hidden behind a curtain of trees and the darkness of night. He tapped the paper against his fingertips. "I'd better have a talk with her."

"Right," Gabe said, looking away. He didn't seem at all surprised or happy by that answer. "Tell me something: Are you planning to be at the Ridge at all today? Because there's only three days left until the Hunt and—"

"I know how many days are left," Colton snapped, and instantly regretted it. None of this was Gabe's fault. The security of both the pack and the territory had a lot riding on whether or not he brought down a Bride this year. For all that he couldn't seem to stop thinking about Karly, he couldn't forget the importance of that either.

"Have you picked out a prospect yet?" Gabe snapped back. "Two would be better than one, although I'd be happy to know you've got at least one *volka* in mind. What pack is she from? Have you talked to her, asked her name, made your intentions known so when you tackle her to the ground, she doesn't chew your face off the minute your weight hits her back? Because in case you're not aware, a lot of folks left the Ridge last night with the very distinct impression that you've suddenly developed a hankering for *chelovak* tail. *I* might just be one of them!"

Throwing back his head, Colton glared through the darkness of crisscrossing tree branches to the star-studded sky above. He kept the explosion of off-color words locked fast behind his clenched teeth. "I know my duty," he said tightly. "I'm getting this lecture from Margo, I don't need it from you too."

"Are you sure?"

The dam holding back his temper cracked just a bit. "What have you got against Karly?" he demanded. "Either of you! Any of you!"

"She's not one of us!" Gabe growled, frustration putting more force behind his words than the situation might otherwise have deserved.

"Half the population of Hollow Hills isn't 'one of us'! Marcus isn't one of us, but you're damn eager to adopt him!"

"At least Marcus is *volka*! But trust me, the day you announce you want to have puppies with him, I guarantee I won't be any happier about his adoption."

Giving him a scathing look, Colton stalked a few paces away before he did something both impulsive and hard to forgive. He didn't have time for this. He ducked past Gabe, heading for the driver's side of the truck to get his clothes out from under the seat. Already the sun was beginning to light up a gray and cloudy sky. It would be dawn soon, and if Karly followed her usual habits, she'd be up and looking for 'Puppy'—he grimaced—within the hour.

Gabe moved away from him too, obviously struggling with his own need to avoid lashing out.

"She doesn't deserve this. She hasn't done a damn thing wrong." Stepping into his uniform trousers, Colton tried to keep his voice even. He pulled them up over his lean hips, adjusting himself in the crotch before zipping his fly. "Other than getting beat up and accidentally hitting me with her car—"

"Oh, that's got nothing to do with this and you know it!" Gabe exploded. "She's human. She's got no loyalty here. She could talk!"

"That's bullshit, and you know it! Karly doesn't talk. She doesn't talk to anyone." Colton shoved his feet into his boots, and then smacked his own chest as he added, "She doesn't even talk to me unless I'm shifted."

"She'll talk—women talk. They always do. Hollow Hills is one word to the wrong person away from starring in an episode of Mountain Monsters!"

Pulling his white tee over his head, Colton shrugged into his uniform shirt and quickly fastened up the buttons. "You want me to walk away, pretend I didn't see this…" He shock the BOLO before shoving it into his back jeans pocket. Dressed once more, he slammed the truck door shut. "…or worse, pretend like I don't care that she's in trouble? If this was anyone from Hollow Hills, not a single person in this town would expect me to turn my back! Well, I'm not turning my back. She came to me; I'm keeping her." He felt a stab of heat burn first into his gut and then rush up through him to fill all the hot corners of his face when he realized what he'd said. "Safe," he added belatedly. "I'm keeping her safe."

Gabe locked his gaze with Colton's, not at all convinced. Still, he dropped his gaze first, already shaking his head in defeat. "I've got a description, so I'll keep an eye out for this stranger. Whoever he is—Whitaker or a private dick—I'll find him."

Colton nodded once, and then turned to follow the road back to Karly's cabin.

"Are you going to mate her?" Gabe called after him. "If you're going to screw everything up, that's fine. I just want to know if I should keep trying."

Colton sighed, his eyes closing, his head rocking back on his shoulders all over again. He turned, throwing out his arms in a helpless, angry shrug. "No Alpha takes a *chelovak*," he said, every word tasting sour in his mouth. "I'll be on the field today and tomorrow; and the day after that, I'm going to run a Bride to ground." That tasted every bit as sour, too. Unable to hold Gabe's knowing eyes, Colton had to look away. "Get Marcus a bunk up at the station until he can find a place of his own. Hollow Hills is ours, and we're not going anywhere."

Gabe just stood there, a grown man with vibes that were bouncing wildly between angry and 'little boy lost'. "If she leaves, you're going to follow her, aren't you?"

"And leave you to be Alpha?" Colton tried to joke, but the argument was too fresh, and both their feelings rubbed just a little too raw.

"That's not what I want," Gabe said.

No, and Colton knew that. What he didn't know was how to soothe the wounds he'd inflicted between himself and his own second. Shaking his head, he ended up walking away, and that wasn't the right thing to do either.

* * * * *

It rained all night long, heavy drops pitter-patting across the tin roof, dripping on it from the canopy of sheltering trees long after the rain actually stopped. Karly had to be getting used to the subtle sounds of country living. Unlike her first night when it stormed, she slept right through the worst of it without so much as a single trace of fear to taint her dreams. Other things, however, did haunt them.

She dreamt of Colton. There wasn't much that she could remember about it once she'd awakened, but his face was right there in her mind and her nipples were peaked, her breasts swollen and heavy, aching for the hands and hot mouth that had, imaginary or not, been attentive upon them. Lying in bed, her sex pulsing molten with a level of desire she hadn't felt in a very long time, she'd squeezed her thighs together, trying to bring back any part of what she'd dreamed, but all she could remember was some hazy sense of being covered, kissed, caressed, and Colton's low voice whispering in her ear, "I'll show you how an Alpha runs his bitch to ground."

When McQueen had said that to her, it had made her skin crawl. But last night, in the fantasy of her dreams, it had felt so very different. It had been possessive, rather than dirty. Seductive rather than derogatory. The way he'd said 'his' had made her feel that way. Like she was his, in every way that mattered.

And now, in the brilliance of the early morning light, Karly tried to make sense of the dream, but already what tantalizing bits that she could remember were dissipating from her mind like thin tendrils of smoke on the wind. Stretching out her arm, Karly felt along the empty sheets beside her, but she already knew what to expect when she opened her eyes. Puppy was gone and, downstairs, the front door was wide open. Whoever had taught him how to open it, Karly grumbled as she crossed the living room, should also have had the decency to also teach him how to shut it. She did it for him, then went back upstairs to shower and gather her dirty laundry.

Without a washing machine and without a clue where the nearest laundromat was, she scrubbed her clothes as best she could in the bathroom sink and hung them up over the shower curtain to dry. She had just headed downstairs to start a pot of coffee brewing and was about to make breakfast when she heard the crunch of truck tires coming up the unpaved road just outside.

Her stomach gave a sickening lurch, one which eased with recognition when she ducked to look out the window and caught her first glimpse of white paint instead of red on the truck that was pulling up to her front porch. It was Colton, coming to check on her again.

Unwanted flashes of last night's dream zipped through her mind, bringing with it a blossom of heat low down in the pit of her stomach. She wished he'd go away. She hadn't yet fully escaped the last man she'd entertained erotic fantasies about. It unnerved her that she was already entertaining fantasies about this one.

He seemed nice enough, some tiny part of her brain pointed out.

He was also big and strong, as well as law enforcement, and that made him too dangerous to risk.

Damn, he was parking instead of turning around.

Double damn, now he was getting out.

Hunkered behind closed drapes, she peeked out through the crack in the curtains, and for a moment, found herself admiring the lazy way he had of walking, sauntering really, all long legs and lean hips, one hand rising to scratch at a corner of his sensual mouth as he climbed the three steps to her door.

Sensual mouth? Really? Karly rolled her eyes, all but groaning at herself.

"Hello," Colton called as he reached the door, offering up a two-knuckled knock to help announce his presence.

Karly frowned. She clutched her hands together, wringing each finger one at a time even as her nipples tightened, stiffening against her will. At least she wasn't afraid of him. He was probably the only person, apart from Mama Margo, that she wasn't afraid of. How pitiful was that?

Colton knocked again. "Miss Smith, can you come to the door please?"

Unsure which was worse, the attraction or the fear, Karly went to the door. Opening it was only half as hard as dragging her gaze away from his smile.

"Good morning," he said softly, his voice as calm and gentle as a cowboy with a skittish mare.

"Good morning," she reluctantly replied.

"You've got power again," he noted.

She glanced back into the kitchen where the light was on and the coffeemaker was just beginning to percolate. The heady aroma was wafting through the cabin and had definitely reached the front door. It would have been polite to offer him a cup, but the intimacy of inviting him in made her hesitate. "It came back on last night."

"You're lucky. Sometimes it takes Montgomery two or three days to get us back on the grid. Hollow Hills is too remote to be on anyone's high priority list."

She looked at the badge on his chest and wrung her hands again, squeezing and choking at her fingers. This was ridiculous. She was ridiculous. Her face felt hot every time she looked at him and, despite the fact that she had a stomach full of strangling knots, there was a tickle of molten awareness flowing down to dampen the folds of her sex.

Damn dream.

She could barely remember it and still it was doing this to her.

"Do...do you want a cup of coffee?" Her voice came out sounding husky, somewhere between a whisper and strangled bedroom arousal that only someone without ears would fail to recognize.

That smile of his broadened, softening his strong features and making that blossom of heat in the pit of her nervous stomach warm all the hotter. "I would love a cup, thank you."

She'd offered; he'd accepted. The die was cast, and her fate was sealed.

She turned and somewhat stiltedly walked back to the kitchen. She found two cups, the only two she had among the meager store of dishes in Margo's mostly empty cupboards.

"Settling in, I see."

Karly jumped at how near his voice sounded. Oh God, he'd come inside!

Well, of course he'd come inside. She'd offered him coffee. She could hardly expect him to stand out on the front porch and chug it. When people were being friendly, they sat at the kitchen table and sipped slowly over civilized conversation.

She couldn't believe she was doing this, and why? Because she'd had a crazy sex dream, that's why. Her hands shook, but she managed to fill both mugs without spilling. "I don't have cream or sugar."

"I don't mind black."

She waited for him to select a chair and then set one of the cups in front of him before taking the chair opposite him. It was the farthest that her tiny kitchen and even tinier table would allow her to get. She cupped her coffee in both hands but didn't drink. She was shaking so badly, she was afraid she'd scald her own lap if she tried. So she sat there, helplessly frozen and staring expectantly back at him.

Bless him, his smile never wavered. He simply sat across from her, waiting for the coffee to cool enough to drink, a large man folded into a relatively small area and so obviously trying his best not to look intimidating.

"So, how are you and Puppy getting along?" he asked.

She looked down at the empty food dish that he'd walked right past on his way to the table. "Fine. Did you see him outside? Sometimes he likes to take walks in the mornings."

"Oh, I'm sure he's around. He likes you."

Karly blinked at him. "How would you know that?"

"He wouldn't still be here if he didn't."

That made sense. Despite herself, she relaxed a little. "I suppose considering your job you know all the strays around here."

"Each and every one," he replied. "But I wouldn't call him a stray. He's just not…owned."

"Isn't that the very definition of a stray?"

"It is, and it would apply…*if* he was a dog."

Her eyebrows beetled together. "He is a dog."

"No, he's a wolf." Colton thought about it, and then amended. "Half wolf, on his father's side. Does that make you nervous?"

Yes.

"If he's half-wolf then someone must have tamed him. He's been very gentle with me."

"That's because his other half is pure good, old-fashioned gentleman." Colton hazarded his first hot sip of coffee, and then amended himself again. "From his mother's side. And, he likes you."

When he smiled at her, Karly caught herself on the brink of returning it. She quickly looked away, afraid of becoming too unguarded in his presence.

"Don't worry. None of the—" Colton lowered his cup, his infectious smile broadening into a grin. "—strays around here have ever bit anyone who didn't first do something to deserve it."

"Is that why you came out here this morning? To tell me they won't bite?"

"Nope." For the first time, his smile dimmed. "I just wanted to make sure you knew Puppy's the one to stay close to if something should happen. The others will follow his lead."

She could already feel herself tensing up again. "If something like what should happen?"

Colton shifted in his seat, and it made her even more nervous when he abruptly set his cup aside to face her fully. "I have to show you something, but first I want you to promise me that you won't let it scare you."

That right there scared her.

"All right." She was proud of herself that, while her soft voice did shake, she didn't sound anywhere near as panicked as she felt.

Setting his coffee to one side, Colton reached into his back pocket and pulled out a folded piece of white paper. He slid it across the table to her, two fingers pinning it to the rickety wooden surface while he reiterated, "Anything you don't understand, I'll be happy to explain. This is nothing you need to be afraid of. It's just something you need to know."

Karly reached for the paper like it was a snake. Her fingers didn't feel quite right, but she still managed to unfold it without too much fumbling. However, their slight tremble became a volatile shaking once she started reading.

"Karly?"

She couldn't breathe. She dropped the BOLO on the table, snatching her hands back and crushing them against her chest to keep from having to touch it. She sucked in a ragged breath, but honestly could not get air into her chest.

"Karly!" Colton's strong voice cut through the panic, reminding her that she wasn't alone.

He wasn't smiling any more. His eyes were grim, locked on hers, and yet somehow he wasn't anywhere near as threatening as that paper lying between them. "This is not a warrant. You're not going to be arrested, and you're not wanted for questioning. All this is, is a missing person's. It's like a picture on a milk carton, okay? And I've already taken care of it."

"Taken care of it?" she echoed. Her throat wasn't working any better than her lungs were. She really did sound strangled now. "What does that mean? How?"

"I had a call placed to the sheriff a couple of towns over. He's a fishing buddy of mine. He's going to cancel this out in a way that won't be traced back to Hollow Hills. You're safe here, sweetheart. You're also not a child. Adults can go "missing" whenever they want to. Do you understand?"

"Yes." She sounded unbelievably calm. Much more so than she felt.

Ducking his head, Colton studied her closely, and judging by that slight narrowing of his eyes, he didn't believe her act. "Do you want to talk about it?"

"No." She didn't mean to snap, but that's how it came out. Hard and bitter sounding.

"Hey."

She didn't want to look at him. She was too afraid of what he might be able to see if he kept looking at her this way. After a moment, he gave up waiting for her to give him a response and gave her one instead. His hand was as firm as it was gentle when he leaned across the table and captured her chin, forcing her eyes back to his. "You're going to be fine."

She almost laughed at him. "You don't know him, so you can't know that."

"Yes, I can. Hollow Hills is my town, not his." Abandoning his chair, Colton came around to her side of the table. He hunkered down, bringing himself to her level. His very nearness should have been threatening, but for some odd reason, Karly didn't find it scary at all. Perhaps because she was already too frightened to feel anything more. "If he's stupid enough to come here, I promise you, he's going to find me a hell of a lot faster than he finds you. Now, I know you've got no reason to, but I hope you'll trust me."

She didn't think she had it in her to trust anyone, especially not now. But then, for whatever reason, he went from looking at her to looking at her mouth, and suddenly everything that Karly wanted most—to run, to find another town, another place to hide—it all shifted. A pulse of wanting strong enough to echo what she had felt in her dream thumped way down deep inside her. She looked at his mouth too, wondering if the reality of being kissed by him would feel as good as it had in her dream.

As if any kiss could possibly ever banish one really big mistake and the four years' worth of hell that had followed.

Her breath caught in the back of her throat, sheer anticipation making it impossible to swallow. His hand on her chin began to wander, his thumb passing once over the bow of her trembling lips before he, incredulously, pushed himself away. He backed away, leaving her unkissed, and Karly honestly didn't know whether to be disappointed or relieved.

"Go, get ready," Colton said, gesturing toward the stairs.

Confused now, Karly didn't move. "For what?"

"You've hidden in this house long enough. I'm taking you out."

CHAPTER EIGHT

It wasn't yet ten in the morning when Colton drove Karly up to the Ridge, but already the parking lot was full. A line of cars wound a good half mile on every available stretch of shoulder from the summit of the Ridge all the way down to the main road. Although they eventually did find a place to park, it was not in the shade and the summer sun was beating down hot enough to soften the blacktop. When she slid down out of his pickup, her first step on it sounded sticky and just up the hill, the road actually seemed to smolder. If there were contenders on the field already, then it was hard to imagine the day ending without at least one really good case of heat stroke.

Only the slightest of mercy breezes brushed through the grass and trees, making the leaves rustle and the branches above them sway. Colton cracked the windows and locked the doors, and then they started walking uphill. Although close enough to hold hands, she was careful to make sure they didn't touch.

"So, is this an annual town celebration?" she asked, trying to fill up the silence with something other than her awareness of the heat—both of the day and of him. They had an uphill hike of only half a mile to go, but she was going to be sweaty, hot and miserable by the end of it. She was also pretty sure they had already passed more parked cars than there were residents of Hollow Hills. She read a nearby license plate. "Montana? Wow. People come from all over, huh?"

"Not always." Seeming not to mind either the heat or the uphill climb, Colton slowed his step to accommodate her shorter legs. "It's more of a regional thing, although people have been known to come from even further away—other countries, even—to attend a Hunt. It's not annual either. One is rarely hosted in the same place twice within any fifty-year span. And although we do sometimes have them every year, it can also skip two or three years or happen within two or three months. It just all depends."

"On what?"

He shot her a quick sideways glance, quirked an equally quick half-smile, and then returned his gaze to the road ahead. His subsequent chuckle was an awkward, self-deprecating sound. "Several things."

That roused her curiosity. "Is it a town secret?"

He caught his breath, an inward laugh that didn't quite make it out far enough to involve sound. At least not until he cleared his throat. "All right. It depends on how often an Alpha needs a Bride."

There was that word again. She thought about it. "So, these are wedding games?"

"Close enough."

"For who?"

He looked away again. "For me, hopefully."

Karly almost stopped walking. She tried to tell herself that sharp stabbing sensation in the pit of her stomach was due to surprise. "Who are you marrying?"

His smile turned every bit as self-deprecating as his laugh had been. "I don't know yet."

"You've never met her…or she hasn't been determined?"

"Both would be accurate."

That surprised her all over again, but this time it did so without that sickening clench to her mid-region. "You said hopefully. Does that mean your marrying is…uncertain?" When he nodded, she asked, "Why?"

"You're asking a lot of questions." He was still smiling when he said it.

"Do you want me to be quiet?"

He laughed softly, shook his head once and then took a deep breath. "It's not certain, Karly, because I'm not the only one vying for the position of Alpha of Hollow Hills. And it's even more uncertain because other packs are trying to take control of this territory and throw us out of it. My catching a Bride won't exactly guarantee my position or prevent an invasion, but it would go a long way toward solidifying my right to defend my position."

"The Alpha male of Hollow Hills?" She tried not to laugh because for all that it sounded silly coming out of her mouth, both he and Mama Margo had used that word quite seriously. "All right, so what does an Alpha do?" She couldn't resist knocking on her chest and offering a sedate Tarzan yodel.

Colton laughed again, and for the second time said, "Close enough."

"No, I'm sorry. I'll be serious. I'm curious. Besides "catching" his Bride—which stirs up a whole slew of new questions, by the way—what does an Alpha do?"

Having rounded a curve in the road, Karly could see the summit of the Ridge up ahead. They weren't close enough yet for her to glimpse the tents through the trees or the colorful pennants, but she could hear the shouting and the laughter and the occasional snap of cloth in the breeze.

"We lead," Colton answered, his expression seeming to close the nearer they drew to the crowded fairgrounds. "We guard our territories." He looked at her then. "And we protect all those within it."

The implication of what he was trying not to say wasn't lost on her. Karly flushed, a slow burning heat that moved up from her core to scald her cheeks. She had to change the subject. "And you decide who gets to be Alpha via ragtag games of tackle football?"

"No." For the first time, his flash of a smile seemed genuine. "The games are simply a means to an end. It gives you a chance to show off your strength to potential females, and if you're lucky, you can also knock a few of your competitors out of the running."

"Is that what you were doing yesterday with that boy?" Having finally reached the summits' intended parking lot, they stepped off the road together, gravel crunching under both their feet.

"That's what he was trying to do to me."

Despite the veiled ruthlessness that she had witnessed yesterday, Karly liked walking beside him. She liked hearing the crunch of his boots grinding in the loose rock and she liked feeling the heat of him, even hotter than the surrounding sun, every time his arm bumped lightly into hers. On the few times when he pulled a little ahead of her, she really liked watching him walk. That swaggering strut of his struck her as sexy. He didn't even seem to know how sexy that was, and that appealed to her, even though she knew it shouldn't.

"So what's on the agenda today? More football and beating each other up?" Karly stopped when he did, but while he stared off toward the banners and tents, she continued to study him.

"Not today," he said softly, and then began to smile. "Sounds like they've got something else planned."

Karly tried to hear what he was, but it was just shouting and cheering. To her, it said football game, but as they approached the same grassy field where Colton had tackled and been tackled the day before, instead of teams of men beating each other into the ground, today it was the women's turn. In this case, the term "the gentler sex" seemed to hold no meaning.

"Oh whoa," Karly said, trying hard not to sound judgmental. Just as the men had done the day before, the contestants were engaged in a rowdy game of skins versus skins. Some were wearing sports bras, but most hadn't bothered, and all of them wore dirt and bruises from no-holds-barred tackles to the ground regardless of who had the ball. "These are your Bridal choices?"

Colton grinned. "I do love our old, time-honored traditions, don't you?"

Karly's startled laugh cut into a wince when four women collided and the one on the bottom of the pile came up bloodied, spitting teeth and grass, and with an arm that bent in ways no human arm should. "Oh wow, these girls are serious."

"Deadly," Colton agreed. "They have a lot to prove. Strong women attract strong mates."

"So does a good curry."

Colton chuckled. "Fond as I am of curry, a woman's cooking skills aren't half as important as strength, courage and good family ties. There are a lot of men here competing for Brides and not one of them is going to care how well she cooks."

Another bone-crushing tackle resulted in two women picking themselves up off the ground. Both spat blood, but only swiped their mouths and rejoined the next line up. This was not hair-pulling, bitch-slapping, name-calling, feminine warfare. This was every bit as brutal as the men had been the day before.

"This has Bridezillas beat all to hell and back," Karly said flatly, and then looked at him. "You want to marry one of these women?"

His smile dimmed around the corners of his mouth. He inclined his head. "Want doesn't have anything to do with it. But yes, in three days' time, we will have our Hunt and I will take one of these women for my Bride."

He did not look happy about it. Funny, but she kind of felt a little disappointed too. She wasn't even fully divorced yet. She didn't have a right to feel like this.

Karly faced the field and tried to study his options with an unbiased eye. "But you don't know which one?"

"No."

"Then why do it?"

"Because it's our way."

The look she flashed him now was all but annoyed. "Oh, come on. What are you, gypsies?"

"Not exactly." He made no effort to change his answer.

Karly cringed when the ball was hiked and two walls of shouting women collided. It might have been simply the sound of the impact, but she thought she heard bones snap. "Oh my God." She tried to cover her eyes, but couldn't make herself stop watching. "What if you don't suit? Apart from potential chest sizes, what do you know about any of these women?"

"I know they care about our traditions." Colton glanced at her sidelong. "I know they are fierce and determined enough to suffer pain in the hopes of attracting my attention. And I know that they will bring that determination into our marriage, because no one wants to be miserable with the one they have vowed to share the rest of their life."

Karly flinched again, but this time it had nothing to do with what was happening before her. "What if you are miserable?"

"Then we'll separate. We aren't perfect, but we aren't draconian either."

Another hike of the ball resulted in another bone-jarring tackle, this time punches were thrown and she could have sworn one girl bit another. Karly folded her arms across her chest, hugging herself against an answer she, for some reason, didn't really want to know. "If you have to pick, have you at least whittled down your options?"

A ghost of his former smile returned. Colton faced the field, folding his arms across his chest now too. "Sadly, I haven't dedicated the proper attention to even begin my whittling. My...family is not at all pleased with me."

"Your family has to approve of her too?"

"At this point, they won't care just so long as I get one. Any one." He didn't sound happy about that, either.

"Okay." Karly studied the field. She pointed to a blonde, her long curly hair pulled back in a ponytail and her bouncing breasts covered but pertly outlined by the wife-beater t-shirt she wore. "How about that one?" She tried her best not to think about Colton covering that woman the way she's dreamed he'd done to her the night before.

"Not if you paid me," Colton said flatly.

That drawling rejection made her so ridiculously happy that she actually smiled. "Why not?"

"Her father's been trying to get his hands on Hollow Hills for years. He failed at brute force, so now he's trying through diplomacy."

"And if you married her, he'd as good as succeed," she concluded. "I didn't realize politics were also involved."

"Politics are always involved," Colton informed her.

"All right." Karly studied the field again, taking her time now to pick and choose among the competing hopefuls. "What about that one?"

"The brunette with the dragon tattoo?" He snorted when she nodded. "She's barely more than a child."

"She's old enough to have a tattoo," she pointed out.

"I'm thirty-eight. I don't want a Bride I'll have to spank and send to bed without supper."

Karly quickly bit back another smile. "All right, so one of the older ladies."

"Not too old," he corrected, his eyes now sparkling with amusement as well. "I don't want to push her wheelchair quite yet either."

"No toothless, old biddies," she agreed and scanned their options. She'd been trying to steer clear of the shirtless ones, but feeling emboldened now, she chose one. "That one, the short-haired blonde."

"She's being particularly aggressive," Colton noted.

"She does seem very strong. And if she's not thirty, then she can't be far from it, so no spanking required."

"More's the pity. She's got the perfect backside for it—nice, round and jubbly."

That caught her so off-guard, that Karly actually whapped him on the arm as she laughed. Colton made no effort to retaliate, but flashed that good-natured grin instead. In spite of herself, Karly relaxed even more. "I can't believe you just said that. All right. So, she's strong, grown, has a nice butt, and since she's running around in public without her shirt on, we'll just assume for now that she's open to kinky sex. All that's left is to find out what her family is like."

"I have no idea; never met them."

"Have you talked to her yet?"

"Enough to know she has a nasally laugh."

"So, you want a strong, older woman from a good family, into kinky sex, but without the nasally laugh."

"Is that asking too much, do you think?" He bumped his shoulder to hers, lowering his head in conspiratory humor, which made her feel as if he were trying to get intimately closer. She liked that too.

"I think you'd be better off looking for someone who makes a good curry."

Grinning, he shook his head and turned from the field to give her his whole attention. "I like this."

"What?" She kept her eyes on the ball game and pretended she couldn't feel herself blushing. It was infinitely safer than looking back at him.

"You. Relaxed and bantering with me."

The heat beating down on her head and shoulders was nothing compared to the slow flush of warmth that spread up from her belly and out through all the rest of her. She shouldn't like the way he was looking at her, but she did. Looks like that had the power to melt a girl from the inside out, and Karly was no exception.

"You shouldn't do that." Unable to continue standing so close to him, she turned and started walking toward the tents.

Not about to be left behind, Colton fell into easy step alongside her. "What shouldn't I do?"

"Look at me like that."

"Why not?" he challenged.

She huffed, a soft breathy laugh that hovered between self-depreciating humor and regret. "Because I'm not..." like them, she almost said—all those young and nubile, pretty and carefree, big- and even bare-breasted women out there on that combatants' field. "I'm not one of your candidate Brides. I'm not what you need."

Colton stopped walking, and after a few steps, she did too. He'd kept his smile, but his eyes had narrowed. "How do you know what I need?"

"I don't," she said flatly. "I just know, whatever it is, you're not going to find it in me."

He stepped in closer, coming almost toe to toe. It was likely just the sun she was feeling, but she could have sworn it was his body heat burning through both their clothes and directly into her. "Where will I find it, Karly?"

"With someone who's not damaged."

She shouldn't have said that. Too late, Karly tried to laugh it off. She didn't want to fight. She honestly could not remember the last time she had felt like this—relaxed, comfortable…content—in another person's company. Not since Dan, certainly. The last thing she wanted was to turn this moment into something ugly. "I'm sorry. Let's not…um…"

He was still staring at her, his mouth flat and no longer smiling. In the broad light of day, his eyes seemed more yellow than amber and he held himself stiff and still, waiting for her to finish explaining.

As if she could explain. She wasn't one of his 'hopeful' contestants. She wasn't even another visitor to Hollow Hills, participating in a long-standing, local tradition—however odd it might be. What had he done but try to be nice and take her mind off the problems waiting for her at home? What had she done, but insinuate herself into his problems, as if she had the right? He had to nip this pointless growth before it budded into something awful.

Just walk away. At this point, it was all she could do, but when she tried, Colton caught her arm and pulled her back. And not just back, he pulled her right up to him. Chest to burning chest with him. His other hand swept up to cup her cheek, skimming just under her injured eye. After so many days, the swelling was all but gone and the bright purple and reds had faded into even uglier hues of yellow and brown. She tried not to flinch, but as gentle as his fingers were, she still did when he brushed along the discolored edge before combing back into her hair and gripping tight to prevent her retreat.

She wasn't at all prepared to fight it when he tipped her head back. There wasn't a single inch of her that wanted to flee the heady heat of his mouth when he captured and kissed her. Right there, in full view of all those women fighting for his attention and the whole of Hollow Hills, watching it unfold. He kissed her like he meant it, rather than like a man simply trying to make a battered woman feel worthwhile again. He kissed her like a man struggling to keep his passion in check, coaxing her with teasing flicks of his tongue until she opened to him, even while the thin line of his restraint trembled just under the strong surface of him.

He moved with her, backing her up until she felt the sudden eclipse of the sun as he moved her into the shade, and then the rough bark of a tree was at her back. He caressed her, soothing her uncertainties one nibble of his mouth at a time, discarding her hesitancies with stroke after wandering stroke of the hand not anchored in her hair. His free fingers forged an exploratory path from her face to her shoulder to her left breast. Her nipples pebbled at the cup of his palm. The sheer heat of him infiltrated into every pore of her, until she could feel her naked want of him pulsing just as hot within her aching womb.

His hips were flush against her hips. His cock, and she could feel it now, prodded at her belly, thick and hard, still safely contained behind the denim of his jeans but making the throb in her sex pulse even deeper.

He released her hair and his hands moved in tandem now, descending to the round curves of her hips, drifting back to grip her buttocks. He squeezed, lifted, bringing her right up onto her tiptoes as he pulled her sex into full contact with his, and that bulge became all she felt. She couldn't imagine any dream more vivid or wonderful than this. She shivered.

Once upon a time, though, Dan had felt this wonderful too.

Colton wasn't Dan, and she knew that. Way down deep in her soul, she knew it. But habits of self-preservation die hard, and just as the wonderfulness of being in Colton's arms pushed her to the brink of wanting to wrap her arms around him neck and maybe even her legs around his hips, her self-preservation kicked in. She twisted and instead of pulling him closer, she shoved, tearing their mouths apart and knocking him back a step.

The bark of the tree scraped up between her shoulders as she landed back on her own two feet, but it was a voluntary retreat on his part, she knew from the way he grudgingly let her go. The amber of his eyes seemed very bright now, alive in a way that felt so very primal.

"I'm married." More than anything right now, she wished she didn't have to explain. "We're getting divorced. He signed the papers, but it's not final yet." She shook her head, even as she edged around the trunk just to get some nerve-settling distance between them again. "But even if it were, I'm still not one of those girls on your field."

Golden fire flashed in the depths of his eyes. His jaw clenched, twice.

"I'm sorry," she whispered. And she meant that too. But being sorry didn't change who she was, who Dan was, and it certainly didn't change Colton.

Hugging herself tightly, desperate to still the snake-like rattling of nerves her sudden depravation of him had caused, Karly made herself walk away. And for a second time, Colton made himself impossible to flee from. He fell back into step beside her. He didn't say anything and he didn't look at her, but there were plenty of other people who did. She could feel their stares. She could all but hear the whispered speculation that followed in their wake. She didn't know any of these people. The censure and speculation she kept glimpsing in these strangers should not have cut her so, and yet, it did. Especially when she noticed Mama Margo watching her from far across the field. She stood near the far cluster of tents where the children and most of the other women had gathered to picnic, keep a watchful eye over the littlest ones, and gossip.

More than a few heads tipped together as sly glances moved from Karly to Colton and then pointedly away whenever they caught Karly looking back at them. The look on Mama Margo's face said everything that Karly didn't need to hear: She wasn't pleased with the attention Colton was paying her. She wasn't pleased because Karly wasn't one of them.

And she never would be.

CHAPTER NINE

Colton bought Karly two coffees over the course of the morning and a chocolate- and raspberry-filled pastry for breakfast. They watched the games, moving from one shade tree to another, following the shadows as the sun reached its zenith and then began to descend again. When one group of women on the field got too tired or too beat-up to continue playing, another took its place and the games started all over again. If there was a score to be kept, Karly couldn't figure it out and Colton didn't volunteer any explanation.

From the thick row of observers in constant motion around the battlefield's outskirts, Karly began to pick out odd groupings among the viewers—certain men kept catching her eye. Maybe it was only because Colton had told her the significance of this town-wide celebration that she noticed them at all, but they were watching so intently, bending their heads together, gathering in peer-aged groups rather than as family units as she would have expected.

"Shouldn't you be out there with the others?" she asked, feeling guilty because it was obvious that she was responsible for keeping him from it. Archaic and somewhat misogynistic though it might be to her; to Hollow Hills this was important, and she had no business judging them.

"I know where I need to be," Colton said, handing her one of three sausages-on-a-stick that he'd just bought from another vender.

"What kind of meat is this?" It smelled spicy and definitely looked homemade.

Colton smirked slightly as he bit into his own. "If you're still curious after you've finished it, I'll tell you. But you probably don't want to know."

Don't get attached, she had to tell herself when he cocked her another of those crooked grins. She knew better than to let herself get drawn in by that sweet, slow, southern boy charm he exuded every bit as effortlessly as he breathed, but, oh, it was so hard. And getting harder the longer she stayed by his side.

The way he took her around the field, introducing her to some of the townsfolk, introducing her to some of the carnival-type games they had set up for those not directly participating in the 'mating' selection going on in the arena—penny tosses, target shoots, pitch and dunks—it began to feel almost like dating. Oh yes, she knew better than this. She should have gone straight home right from the moment she realized she was going to have this problem, but it had been so long since anyone had paid her this kind of attention.

She liked it. She'd missed it. She felt such a surging hatred for Dan, who had robbed her of so much these last four years. On the heels of that, though, came a cascading wave of fear because she knew this wasn't permanent. Colton wanted something she couldn't give him, and all she wanted was to feel safe, if just for a little while.

Colton did that for her. It was ridiculous how secure he'd made her feel in such a shockingly short amount of time. But that didn't mean she should attach herself to him, and since marriage was what he was after, she knew the decent thing to do would be to leave. Free him up to win the notice of one of the women battling for his attention out on that silly field. But, she didn't.

She let him buy her a huckleberry ice slush instead. She even let him put his arms around her on the pretense of showing her how to hold a rifle to hit the metal bottle targets, and she shot that rifle all the while pretending as if she never saw Mama Margo's frown growing more and more pronounced the longer her hawk-eyes watched them. Or that she couldn't see that Colton's Fish and Game companions were frowning too. No matter where they went around the fairground set-up of the Ridge, she kept catching sight of Gabe and another man, his arms sleeved in tattoos, watching in grim disapproval.

What was she doing?

Having a little fun, she tried to tell herself. And why not? Why shouldn't she let herself feel happy for once, even if it wasn't real and only for a little while? Who was she really hurting if Colton was content to shower her with his attention, instead of someone more…available?

Afternoon was well upon them by the time all that coffee and slushies finally caught up with her. Spotting a familiar blue line of port-a-potties set up along the far end of all those colorful tents and flapping banners, Karly excused herself.

"I'll be right here," Colton said, taking up a waiting stance against the base of a sprawling old birch. He raised his hand in hailing salute to someone in the crowd as she moved off, but nature was calling and the call was more insistent than her curiosity over whoever might be moving in now that she had left his side.

Although arguably some of the nicest biffies she'd ever had the pleasure of enthroning herself in, it was while Karly was laying down a toilet paper barrier around the plastic seat that she heard the first disparaging remark.

"I don't know. She showed up just before the Hunt."

"Is she competing?"

"Don't be stupid. She's *chevolak*."

Two women laughed. For all that it was light and tinkling, it was an ugly sound.

"If she's not competing, then she needs to get off the Field."

"She's been playing in Alpha Sight all morning. Someone needs to kick her ass and show her the door."

That Karly was the 'she' in question was as plain as the blue of the plastic walls surrounding her. The catty women sounded young; Karly tried not to listen, but they were answering nature's call in the biffies next to her and none of them were making an effort not to be overheard.

"I came a long way for this chance, and I'm not losing it because some *chelovak* slut can't stop waving her tail under *volka* noses."

"The Alpha McQueen was sniffing for her yesterday."

"She can have McQueen. It's the Alpha Lauren I want."

Karly quickly finished what she had to do, hoping to slip away before the other women noticed her. Unfortunately, all three vacated the port-a-potties at the same moment, and when they saw her, the awkwardness of the silence that followed suddenly felt as heavy as the sun was stifling hot. Karly made herself smile.

"Excuse me," she said, and tried to walk away.

Recovering from her surprise first, the dark-haired woman to her immediate right stepped back and would have let her slip past without another word. But the blonde beside her moved to plant herself directly in Karly's path.

"You heard me and I meant every word," she said flatly. "Get your tail down, bitch, or I'll pin it down for you."

Her dark-haired friend tried to intervene. "Mama Margo said—"

"Mama Margo can lick my piss," the blonde cut her off. Her amber eyes locked on Karly again, a corner of her mouth twisting in a chilling smile. "So can you, little *chelovak*. Run along home, before you get hurt."

Confrontation had never been Karly's strongest trait. The urge to do just that—to run—shivered right up her legs. She tried to push past her, but although the blonde woman did step aside to allow it, she only made a handful of steps before the blonde planted a hand in the middle of Karly's back and shoved. Karly landed in the dirt and grass on her hands and knees. The blonde didn't laugh, but other people did, and suddenly that shiver that rocketed up her spine changed. It wasn't fear, it was raw red fury that stabbed into the back of her head and raised every fine hair on her neck and arms with the prickling need to just unleash.

Was this what Dan felt just before he'd slap her? Karly watched her hands balling into fists in the dirt and grass, nowhere near as appalled as she was angry.

No way was she about to get into a fistfight right outside the portable toilets.

Karly got up. Only by supreme effort did she resist the all but overwhelming urge to turn around with all the knuckles of her tightly-clenched fist leading the way. She started walking again, trailed by sniggers and whispers. People gave her looks, but they moved out of her way.

Colton was still waiting where she'd left him, talking with his Fish and Game co-workers, but she had no intention of rejoining him. From the corner of her eye, she saw him glance her way when she ducked through the crowd and under the ropes of the sectioned off football field. She saw Margo too. The old woman straightened, her frown deepening when she spotted Karly. She held up a silencing hand, and the two grandmotherly women holding court beside her abruptly stopped talking and both turned to stare at Karly as she ducked under the pennant laced rope that sectioned off the football-*cum*-battlefield.

She headed straight for the rows of women lining up against one another.

"Team's full," the shirtless woman currently holding the ball snapped when Karly neared her. "Get off the f—"

Apart from being rude, she hadn't done one thing to earn the broken nose that Karly gave her, effectively 'tagging' her out of the game. The other players stared, some startled, others bristling, but Karly stepped right over their fallen comrade and took the ball away from them all. Tucking it under her arm, Karly walked far enough away from both teams to claim a clear space of open field.

Mama Margo was watching intently now, her eyes wide and her mouth slowly curling at the corners. Gabe nudged Colton, pointing to her, and when Colton turned around, although Karly was too far away to hear him, one didn't have to be a lip-reader to make out the four-lettered curse that fell from his startled mouth.

"Oh shit," he said, his eyes going wide.

Karly turned, locating the blonde who had rejoined a group of friends, all women, all watching her through narrowed eyes and from behind smirking, mocking smiles. Those smiles faltered when Karly pointed right at them. She gave them a single-finger salute, and they looked at one another.

"What are you doing?" a woman from just behind her asked.

When Karly looked back, she found the woman she'd just hit standing at her elbow, her dark eyes bright with curiosity and something that looked suspiciously like humor. Blood still trickled from her nose, though she absently swiped at it with the back of her hand.

"You might want to back up," Karly told her. "This probably isn't going to go well."

"Probably?" the woman echoed, then snorted. "You know who that is, don't you, *chelovak*? That's the Alpha Deacon's daughter, and the only thing she's 'probably' going to do, is kill you. You realize that, yes?"

The blonde was already inside the roped off section of field with her smirking entourage fast at her heels when Karly turned back around.

"She's going to try." Karly tried again to find a nice open space between herself and the other women in which to get her ass handed to her. She wasn't a fighter. She'd fought back in self-defense once or twice, but beyond that, the only punch she'd ever thrown in her life had been the one that had connected with the woman now trailing her.

"No one will stand with you, *chelovak*," she was saying. "You realize *that* too, yes?"

"Sorry about your nose," Karly told her, giving the ball a careless toss behind her. The Deacon girl was not coming to play a game and it seemed silly to continue holding the thing.

"I've been tickled harder than you hit." Snorting again, the woman looked at Karly speculatively, then the blonde who was almost upon them, and then back at the two teams of women, standing back to watch. Most seemed darkly amused. Others were more stoic, their dismissive air betraying how offended they were by her very presence.

"What the hell," the woman said, sliding into a defensive posture next to Karly.

"What are you doing?" Karly asked.

"Like I'm going to let a *chelovak* have all the fun," she shot back, with a lift of her chin and a narrowing of her eyes. "I never could stand this bitch anyway. I'm Maya."

"Karly," Karly returned, hunkering down beside her. On the opposite side of that rope fence, it had taken four men to prevent Colton from coming to her rescue. There wasn't a single space to be seen anywhere among the other spectators. Whole families had assembled to watch her skirmish with the Deacon's ill-mannered daughter, and just enough time had passed now that Karly's initial flush of anger had faded and common sense was striving hard to regain control. The only reason she wasn't trying to think of a way to back out of this was that smugly hostile smile the blonde was wearing.

"Is that a C or a K?" Maya whispered with a funny half-panting laugh. "I want to make sure I spell it right for your obituary."

In spite of what was coming, Karly smiled. "K. And thanks. Now I really am sorry I hit you."

With a warrior's yell, the blonde suddenly charged and all her friends came with her. It was five against two, but it may as well have been against one for all the attention they paid to Maya. Karly had no idea what she thought she was going to prove, but they hit her hard enough to take her straight to the ground—planting a knee in her ribs, smashing her face into the dirt until she could taste blood in her mouth.

They stayed on top of her, pinning her under a mighty weight of hands and knees, ripping at her hair in the subsequent struggle to keep her head in the grass while, above her, the Deacon's blonde daughter unzipped her pants, squatted down right there in front of the entire fair, and pissed on Karly's back.

"You're my bitch now," she cooed, the cruel mirth dancing feral in her silken voice.

All the hands released Karly at the same time. Fury and humiliation helped her get up, and it was an ugly jeering cheer that ripped through the crowd when she stripped off her soiled shirt. She'd have taken her pants off too, but they weren't as wet and didn't smell as strongly of urine as her top did. And she still had some tattered shreds of pride left.

"Go, *chelovak*," the blonde told her, waving dismissively as she turned away. "While you can still walk."

Karly threw her urine-soaked shirt, hitting the blonde dead in the back of the head. She barely waited for her opponent to rip the shirt off her back before she charged. Dimly, she was aware of Maya laughing. It was still five against two, and she'd only just started her attack when the blonde snapped back around. The two women collided and although Karly had the advantage of momentum, the blonde still knocked her down, flat on her back this time. With three of her four friends landing quickly on top of Karly to help hold her down, she crawled up Karly's frame, growling and drawing up a mouthful of snot to spit. Karly jerked up her knee, slamming with all the force she could muster and nailing a direct hit between the blonde's splayed legs.

The force she'd used would have crippled a man, but the Deacon's daughter, while hurt, was only stunned long enough for Karly to shove out from under her. She elbowed one woman in the neck and Maya knocked the other two off, pulling Karly free of the pile.

The blonde came up off the ground with teeth gritted and her eyes holding nothing but fury. "I am going to kill you," she hissed.

Karly smirked. "You can try, anyway."

"I think you must be insane," Maya said, when Karly lined up alongside her for the next charge. "You do realize they were only playing with you before, yes?"

From the look on the blonde's darkly seething face, playing wasn't what they would be doing now. She erupted with another warrior's bellow as she and her crew charged, and Karly knew a split second of exhilaration right before the bone-jarring impact knocked her flat on her back. She felt the punches then, the kicks and slaps, and then everything exploded into pain.

* * * * *

Mama Margo took Karly's hand, turning it palm up and slapped a huge steak into it. The entire time she'd been at the cutting board, mercilessly tenderizing it with a mallet, rolling it in herbs and buttermilk and more herbs before beating it all over again, she hadn't said a word. She didn't say anything now, either. She just gave Karly a bemused look, her lined mouth curling at the corners, but there was a world of censure drifting through those aged eyes. Karly had never felt so scolded in all her life.

Herb-dotted buttermilk dripped between her fingers as Mama Margo pushed her hand and steak both up to her blackened eye. The left one now. Her lip was split in two places and she was hosting a world of bruises in hundreds of dully aching places that ran the gauntlet of her body from head to toes. Nothing was broken. At least, she was familiar enough with what past broken bones felt like that she didn't think anything was now. She knew she'd been lucky. That, and she had a sneaking suspicion that, in spite of her obvious anger, the Deacon's blonde daughter and her friends hadn't had a chance to pummel her too long before the savage arrival of one very big, very black and very pissed-off wolf.

Snapping and snarling, Puppy launched himself into the fight like a massive, four-legged, pointy-eared and sharp-toothed knight to the rescue. His attack sent the blonde and her malicious friends scattering, though they didn't go far.

"She's *chelovak*!" the Deacon's daughter snapped, as if Puppy would even care. He stood over her, head down, hackles up, every breath he took a seething in- and exhaling growl. Karly had never seen an animal look, act or sound more vicious. That he didn't actually bite anyone only went to prove how truly gentle he was, despite his wolfish half. As she'd lain dazed and bleeding in the grass, fighting to keep her eyes open and focused, all Karly could do was reach up and twine her fingers in the soft fur of his neck ruff. She might have blacked out a little then, because the next thing she knew, suddenly there were snarling, snapping wolves all around her.

Who let the dogs out, her brain tried to sing. It was all she could do not to get stepped on as two grey wolves dashed in to nip at Puppy's tail and flanks. Fighting to stay on top of her, covering as much of her prone body as he could, Puppy snapped back. A wolf grabbed her shoe, jerking hard as if to pull her out from under him, but Karly was instantly released when Puppy turned on him. But turning gave the two wolves at his back an opportunity for attack and they took it, snapping at his flanks all over again.

Karly tried to get up, to protect him from the teeth coming at them from every side, and suddenly it seemed the whole field exploded in growling, barking, and aggressive wolves. Two more, a grey and tan, charged through the hostile pack that surrounded them. They tore into the wolves nipping after Puppy, sinking teeth into fur and sending half the pack scrambling to break away. But, they didn't flee very far. When they returned, they did so with reinforcements of their own.

Her head spinning, Karly tried to get up again but it was almost impossible with three wolves now standing on top of her, shielding her from the encroachment of hostile animals. She'd been too dazed back then to be scared, that had come later, only minutes later really, when she saw Margo walking through the thick of all that snapping and snarling, delivering cuffs and kicks, and one round-house slap to the muzzle of the blond wolf who dashed in to snatch at Karly's shoe again, tugging and jerking to wrest her out from under her protectors. Mama Margo knocked that wolf belly-to-the-ground.

"Best behavior," she shouted down at the grudgingly cowering wolf. When she turned sharp yellow eyes on the rest of the massive pack, they all fell silent. Many began slinking away. "I meant it when I said it, and I mean it still! Get off with ya! All of you!"

By the time she'd reached Karly's side, Karly was feeling sick to her stomach. Her head wouldn't stop spinning. She reached for a helping hand, except Mama Margo did not extend one.

"Get up," she'd said instead, though not unkindly. "Follow me. Do it under your own power, or they'll never respect you."

She probably meant the townspeople, but all Karly could see around her were wolves. Then again, her eyes weren't focusing well. At that point, it had been all that she could do just to get her feet under her and her legs solid enough to keep her steady. If Puppy hadn't been right there, nuzzling her hip and offering his back for balance, she never would have made it more than a few steps.

Eventually the dizziness passed though, and when it did, Karly found herself being escorted through the parking lot and back down the road to Colton's truck by dozens of—dare she say, friendly?—wolves. Of course, those wolves were followed the entire way by dozens and dozens, a veritable ocean of stalking and snarling unfriendly ones.

She had no idea where Colton had gone. The thick crowd that had been jeering and cheering just minutes ago had dispersed with the arrival of the wolves. At first, Karly thought she might have to walk all the way back to the fairground to find him, but each time she'd tried to turn around, Mama Margo had caught her arm and kept her moving. In the end, a car pulled up beside them.

"Get in," McQueen said, leaning across the seat to shove the passenger door open.

"I have to wait for Colton."

"You have to get home, right now," Mama Margo corrected, frowning at Puppy and then at her. "I'm sure he'll be by when he can."

Her legs were so watery and her head was starting to pound. She wanted to turn around and walk back to the fairgrounds. The problem was, even if there hadn't been so many vicious wolves skulking in cautious circles just beyond Mama Margo, Puppy and those two wolves who'd decided for no apparent reason to be her protectors, she physically didn't think she could.

"Get in," McQueen snapped again.

Unsure if she could keep walking, Karly started to, but Puppy muscled his way in first. He climbed onto the front seat, yellow eyes locked on the driver, growling the whole way.

"Mutts in back," McQueen said, unimpressed.

Puppy not only sat between them on the front seat the entire way home, but he sat facing McQueen, his lupine stare fixed and unblinking. He didn't stop growling once.

"I'm sorry about that," Karly mumbled, feeling each of her teeth to make sure they were all still there and solid in her gums. Her lips felt thick. It made talking feel every bit as funny as it had after one of her husband's attacks.

McQueen just drove, taking those unpaved roads slowly and trying to jostle her as little as possible when avoiding certain potholes became impossible. It was kind of sweet, actually. At that moment, it had been difficult for her to remember why she'd ever found him or his brothers to be such frightening individuals.

"Your breath stinks," McQueen eventually said.

Karly didn't for a second think he was talking to her, but she slung a companionable arm around Puppy's bristling shoulders and said, "I'm sorry about that too."

McQueen slid her a glance, but didn't speak again until they'd passed the ramshackle homes he shared with his brothers and was almost to her driveway. "You've got balls," he finally offered. "I like that in a woman."

She'd probably been punched one too many times in the head, but for some reason, Karly found that too funny not to laugh. The act of smiling made the cuts in her lips split and bleed all over again and laughing hurt her jaw, but she couldn't help it. She hugged her side and tried to protect her aching mouth, or at the very least, not to bleed all over McQueen's car, until her giggles turned to groans and then to panting breaths that were just one errant giggle away from becoming laughter all over again. "Thanks."

Eying her sideways, McQueen snorted once himself, but he didn't say anything more until after he'd dropped her off at her porch. Mama Margo arrived just as McQueen was helping her up the steps. The adrenaline was starting to wear off now, and all her lumps, bumps and bruises were beginning to make themselves felt.

"Don't come back to the field," he told her, by way of goodbye.

If she could have walked, Karly's instinct was to make her way immediately right back up to the Ridge. To strut her stuff, so to speak, and show that even as resoundingly bested as she'd just been, she was not beaten.

Several hours had passed since then. Now, sitting in her kitchen with a piece of herb-encrusted meat on her face and buttermilk dripping down her chin, in spite of feeling just a little bit foolish for how she'd behaved, mostly what Karly felt was empowered. She'd never stood up for herself like that before. She hadn't won that fight, not by any means, but she was so proud of herself for being in it, that she felt good. No, better than good. Despite the pain, she felt great.

"Well," Mama Margo asked, cleaning up what little mess she'd made in the preparation of her black-eye poultice. "What have you learned, then?"

"I don't know." Smiling still hurt like hell, but Karly couldn't help it. "Do you think I taught her anything?"

"Do you mean like, crazy isn't as easy to spot as black eyes and blonde hair?"

"I'm definitely going back up there tomorrow," Karly said, laughing all over again when Mama Margo barked hard amusement toward the kitchen ceiling.

Puppy groaned.

"Poor Puppy," Karly cooed, groaning now herself as she eased off the kitchen chair to sit on the floor beside him. She stroked his big head. "I'm making you work too hard, aren't I?"

He didn't look at her. She tried to make amends with scritches behind his alert ears and even bent to drop a kiss on top of his head.

Glancing from one to the other, Margo seemed to soften just a bit. It might have been a trick of the day's fading sunlight though, because once she'd gathered her supplies to go, she was once again every bit the hardened deep-country woman Karly had come to know.

"Fifteen minutes," she said gruffly, gesturing to the meat in Karly's hand.

"Until what?" Karly wanted to get up and follow Margo to the front door. At the very least, that would have been good manners. But she just didn't have the strength to get up off the floor, and Mama Margo didn't seem inclined to wait for an escort.

"Until dinner," the old woman called back over her shoulder on her way out the front door. "Steak's damned expensive and it doesn't do shit for black eyes. Eat it!"

CHAPTER TEN

That night, Karly dreamt that she was stiff and sore, dozing in and out of sleep in her bed while a spring storm raged outside. Lightning flashed and thunder rattled the windows, but it wasn't Puppy lying beside her, keeping the nightmares at bay. It was Colton, and that's how she knew it was a dream. He was naked, wearing only a flickering halo of blue-white lightning coming in through the open window curtains and the brand-new collar she'd had to buy for Puppy, because no matter how hard she looked, she just couldn't find the old one. It had probably got hung up in the woods somewhere, snagged on a branch during his early morning wandering sessions. Or on his mad-dash run to rescue her on the field. How Puppy always seemed to know when she was in trouble, she just didn't know.

Karly looked at Colton, and he, at her; for the longest moment, simply looking at one another. For the first time in a very long time, Karly wasn't afraid. Not even when he raised his hand to touch her face, the feather-light caress of his fingertips brushing stray wisps of hair back from her bruised cheeks.

It felt so real—the realest dream she'd ever had, but that's all it was. And dreams had a way of letting a girl do things she never would have had the courage to otherwise do.

Her hand didn't even tremble when Karly touched him back, the hard angle of his cheek, the strong line of his jaw, down to his chin, up to his lips. He felt so warm. Soft in some places, and hard as rock in others. She lost the fight against an involuntary shiver when his hand moved to her shoulder, caressed down her side, settling at the small of her back where the tips of his fingers began to trace imaginary circles on her skin. When he leaned in to her, Karly didn't even try to pull away. His lips provoked the sweetest of surrenders. She opened to him almost from the very start, and when he shifted, she rolled with him, welcoming the comfortable weight as he eased himself to lie on top of her.

His hands touched her everywhere, traced her everywhere. They followed all the lines of her, his kissing mouth never far behind as if he hungered to taste every inch of her—her neck, her shoulder, her waist. His tongue dipped, flicking twice at her navel before moving lower still. He took her underwear off with his teeth. No one had ever done that to her before, and just when he had her squirming and panting on the sheets, he shifted his direction, following the caress of his hands all the way down the outer line of her legs and all the way back up along the inner sloping curves. The soft pressure of his fingers coaxed her to open to him, until his hands were right there on the inner heat of her thighs, framing the liquid pulse of heat that was her sex.

"Oh my God!" she gasped when he fastened on her, grinding against the mattress, grabbing her pillow and her hair, pulling at both as she writhed to the suckling, lashing motions of his consuming mouth.

She was still married.

It wasn't cheating if it was a dream.

And she was getting divorced anyway, so who the hell cared about Dan?

Karly moaned, undulating up into the pressure of his hot mouth, riding the sweeping lash of his restless tongue while the coils of pleasure rolled and tightened inside her. She arched, catching her breath, her belly tensing, her legs trembling.

"Oh my God!" she cried, and every taut nerve in her body erupted with a release so intense it was almost pain.

He forced her to ride the storm, one rippling, hip-bucking wave after another, until her gasps escalated into cries and suddenly he was climbing her, burning a path of suckling kisses into her as he rose—trailing up her stomach, to the stiffened peaks of each begging nipple, eventually conquering as far as her oh-so tender mouth—to drink her shrill gasp when she felt the solid heat of his erection settle directly against her wanton sex. He was not in her, but he thrust as if he were, dragging back and forth along her folds, letting her feel the length and hardness of him.

"Say my name," he commanded.

God, he sounded so real. He felt so real. Why did this have to be a dream?

"Colton," she first gasped and then shouted when in a single thrust he went from pressing against her to pushing up deep inside her. "Yes! Oh, please yes!"

He rocked the entire bed with the force of his possession, and she loved it. It had been so very long since she had felt the intensity of sex like this. She grabbed, catching his buttocks in both hands, capturing him in the wrap of both legs and pulling him as deeply into her as he would come.

"Please," she begged, her whole body arching up into his next thrust when he growled—that low, delicious sound—into her hungry mouth. "Please!"

He caught her wrists and she didn't mean to, but her nails raked him when he tore her hands from his ass and pinned them to the pillow above her head. The lamp on the bedside table rattled from the force of his pumping. His kisses became nips; her gasps, groans. It was a bad line in a comedy romance, but the headboard actually knocked against the wall and she was barely aware of it when the lamp fell off onto the floor. Every inch of her luxuriated in the feel of him, the dream of him, so fierce in his need of her that he was growling and his eyes were brightening. They were so yellow that she could see the glow of them in the dark.

A flickering flash of lightning briefly lit the room, casting him in a wash of ghostly white and illuminating the bump and grind where their bodies were so fiercely joined. She both saw and felt it when he pulled out of her. In the flicker of the lightning, she only caught a glimpse of her arousal glistening on his standing cock before the shadows reclaimed the room. His eyes stayed yellow though. His exhaling breath seared her shoulder, a lusty growl that made her sex spasm to hold him again.

He flipped her onto her belly, his warm hands scouring caresses up and down her body just before he bit the fleshy hills of her buttocks, first one and then the other. He threw his leg over both of hers and she gasped, arching into the unbelievable rightness of his tongue running up the length of her spine. She scrambled to get her hands and knees under her, to tip her hips back for him even as the burning heat of his cock burrowed between her legs.

Karly thrust her hand down, needing to touch him as he slid inside her again. They both groaned, guttural and raw. His fist locked in her hair, dragging her head back until his mouth claimed hers once more. He wasn't just kissing her now— even passionate kisses were gentle. This was devouring. The steady slap of his hips spanked her ass, punctuating her moans and his growls. This wasn't just sex, either. He was consuming her, possessing her one rigorous thrust at a time, as powerful and unstoppable as the rain that was beating down on the old tin roof. His strong arm around her waist kept her right where he needed her. Her hands twisted in the sheets, clawing as she strove for something grounding to cling to.

It all felt so real—from the shuddering force of the climax that ripped through her, to all the points of his teeth sinking into her shoulder blade as he used her flesh to muffle his escalating grunts before that final violent shove pushed her flat against the mattress. He ground into her, fighting to get as deep as he could. He shook and shook, shuddering out that long, last growl before he sagged on top of her. His breaths burned her throbbing shoulder. His sweat dripped and pooled, mingling with hers in the small of her back.

He felt so very, very real.

"You're the best dream I've ever had," she breathed as he rolled onto his back beside her to catch his breath. "I wish you were really here."

He looked at her, the shadows of surprise illuminated by another flash of lightning already melting into quiet resignation. "Maybe tomorrow I will be." He pulled her closer, tucking her in snug against his chest and wrapping her in arms that felt strong and warm and safe. He stroked her hair. "Sleep."

Her sex pulsing—hot, wet and sated—her eyes drifted closed. She liked the way his breath felt brushing across her neck. The morning might erase it all away, but right here and now, all she felt was how good and right this was.

Somewhere outside, a lone wolf howled. She didn't think it possible to sleep within a dream. She thought she felt it when Colton rolled his head to follow that sound, but by then, she was dozing in and out. His fingers caressed lightly through the tangles of her hair. He might even have kissed her on the forehead, but then he let her go and the mattress faintly jostled as he got up. Her eyelids felt almost too heavy to lift, but she managed to pry them open long enough to watch as, naked, he went to the window. He even looked like a dream: lean and strong and so…primal. His shoulders were so broad; his chest tapered to a narrow waist and lean hips. Muscle after hard muscle flexed as he parted the curtains, rippling in the eerie blue flash of another lightning strike as he peered outside.

He turned his head as that howl came again, closer this time. He listened a moment, then glanced back at her. The shadows must have hid her face better than it did his. Another flash of lightning, a rumble of distant thunder, and then he turned from the window. A strange, melting undulation hunched and twisted him, dropped him to the floor. And then it wasn't Colton at all, but Puppy who trotted from the room on shadow-black and whisper-soft paws.

"You are so fucked," Dan hissed in her ear.

Karly jerked upright, lurching backwards in an eruption of bedding and flailing limbs, her heart jumped up into her throat, colliding with the scream that choked her there as she fell right off Puppy's side of the bed and landed with a graceless 'whump!' on the floor.

Night was gone. It wasn't yet dawn, but there was just enough grayish pre-morning light for her to see she was alone in the room. Puppy was gone. There was no Colton standing naked at the window. Certainly there was no Dan crouched in the shadows at the head of her bed, but it still took a long time for her to calm down enough to stop hyperventilating. It was longer still before she stopped shaking. So much for last night's feelings of empowerment, all she felt now was nervous and sore.

Huddled up against the wall under the window, Karly unfurled. Every single muscle in her body was protesting yesterday's indiscretion and this morning's fall. And where were her clothes? She looked all around the floor. The last time she had slept naked, it had been her third anniversary and not her choice. What a horrible way to end what had been, up until then, a nice, if inappropriate dream.

Picking herself up off the floor, Karly had to remake the bed before she found her nightshirt and discarded underwear wrapped up in the tussled sheets and blankets. The elastic scrape as she pulled her panties up her legs rekindled sleepy memories of how it had felt when Colton had dragged them off her. She'd never had a dream so vivid that she'd kicked her own clothes off before. She'd never had a dream so vivid, period. And her body had definitely reacted. If she hadn't known better, she'd have sworn she honestly had spent the night in Colton's erotic embrace. Her thighs were still sticky and slick, and her shoulder…

Karly reached back, finding a tender spot high up on the back of her shoulder blade. She was tender everywhere though, which was probably why that bite had felt so vivid when she'd dreamed it. Every inch of her ached. Her brain must simply have converted the sensation to make her sleeping imagination all that much more realistic.

She managed to hold that thought right up until she'd made her way to the bathroom. Ugh, she looked awful. The bruise Dan had given her now stood out as old marks amidst all the fresh new cuts, scrapes and purpling weals. She tsked and turned, twisting and arching up on her tip toes in an effort to see as much of herself from behind as the short medicine cabinet would allow.

She had a massive purplish-red circle on the ball of her shoulder and down her arm where she must have blocked some kicks yesterday. A series of crusty scrapes down her spine reminded her of road rash that looked far worse than it actually felt. But then she saw the crescent of tooth-like marks that marred the slope of one shoulder blade. Practically hidden behind her cascade of blonde hair, it stood out against her pale skin in a place that was, as if by some grand design, remarkably void of injury.

Sweeping her hair back and twisting as far as she could, Karly craned to see it better. She tried to touch it, struggling to make out what that mark was, even as her startled brain supplied the ready answer: A love bite. Colton's love bite.

"That's not possible," she whispered, her skin prickling at an echoing approximation of his hands locking in her hair, his five o'clock shadow scraping her flesh a half second before his teeth sank into her.

Her stomach fell all the way to her toes. It was the oddest sensation, that. Could someone have bitten her yesterday and she'd just not noticed at the time? They'd been kicking and pummeling her so ferociously, and she had lost consciousness ever so briefly. It was possible. But as she stared into her own wide eyes, she already knew that wasn't what she believed. Except, what did that then mean? That her dream last night had been…real?

Karly cupped her forehead, stubbornly determined not to go there. Of all the possible explanations—not that there were many—that was the most ridiculous. Colton did not break into her house late last night, and not only slip past Puppy, but replace him in her bed. He certainly didn't cuddle right up behind her, awakening her so erotically that she hadn't startled or even thought it odd when he began to make love to her. And he absolutely did not do all that and then, what? Sneak back out again like some guilty morning-after attempt to flee any chance of commitment or entanglement?

Against her will, her mind shot back to that moment when the lightning had lit up her room just as Colton turned from her window. Karly went from cupping her forehead to cupping her mouth as she remembered again the way he had rippled, melted, shifted right there in front of her eyes, dropping down onto all four legs before trotting from her bedroom in his Puppy guise.

No.

No, that had definitely been a dream. It just…it just wasn't possible for a man to transform into a dog—

Wolf.

—anywhere except on a Hollywood movie screen.

"Don't be stupid," she told herself.

Except that it would explain so much.

"The hell it would."

Like Puppy's ability to open doors.

"Lots of dogs open doors." Cats too. You-Tube and Facebook both were full of such videos.

Like Puppy and Colton never being in the same place at the same time.

Mama Margo yelling at Puppy as if he were a person…

Gabe, leaning against her car, talking to him and that moment when she could have sworn she'd heard Colton talking back, right before she'd rounded the tail of her car and Puppy had popped his head up over the seat to look at her…

A soft thump from downstairs made Karly jump. Her heart was racing, but it took her a moment to realize it had been doing that even before she'd heard that sound. She rubbed her forehead.

"Get a grip, for God's sake," she whispered, both in regards to her absurd thoughts and in her jumpiness. "He's not a…"

A what? A werewolf?

That was just plain crazy.

Another soft bump. Karly felt her stomach tighten, but in the back of her mind, she already knew what that sound was: Puppy, doing his early morning Houdini routine, either letting himself out of the house or trying to get back in again.

Did she really want to go down there and confront him? She could just see herself now, refusing to let him back into the house until he proved he was just a dog and not Colton in disguise.

Shaking her head at herself, Karly jerked her nightshirt on, covering that mark on her shoulder blade, as if banishing it from even accidental sight might somehow rob it of its existence. Leaving the bathroom felt a little like fleeing, but Karly refused to continue standing there, entertaining the most absurd thoughts imaginable.

She hit the bottom of the stairs, turning left into the living room, but the body she suddenly came nose to chest with was much too big and much too human to be Puppy's.

"I've got your divorce papers right fucking here," Dan said, effectively ripping all breathable air right out of her chest. The panic didn't hit until a half second later, a blinding shock of force that had her legs moving before her brain had even fully recognized the danger, when Dan grabbed for her. He didn't have anything in his hands. He didn't even have hands; he had fists.

Karly tried to run back up the stairs, but he grabbed first her nightshirt and then her ankles. She screamed as she fell, landing half on the second floor landing. Her nails scraped the carpet as he dragged her back down the stairs on her belly, whacking her chin on the corner of the topmost step as she went over it, hands flailing to grab anything with which to anchor herself.

When she hit the living room floor, she tried to roll over, but Dan had already shifted his grip, abandoning her legs to seize her by the hair. Karly grabbed his hand in both of hers just to keep from being scalped as he dragged her around the tiny living room, content for the moment just to make her crawl.

"You think you can humiliate me in front of everyone and then just walk away? Oh no, babe. 'Til death do us part. That's what you promised me, and that's what I'll fucking have!"

He flung her like a ragdoll against the wall. Karly grabbed blindly, catching hold of his belt as she fell, and he slapped her. Her ears rang. Everything spun. When she saw his hands coming at her, she slapped back, but he still grabbed her throat in both hands, slamming her to the floor as he squeezed and pinning her there.

Sucking but unable to find the air, Karly clawed at his fingers. The weight of him pressed down on her chest. No matter how she kicked and bucked, she couldn't dislodge him. He just squeezed harder until spots of bright light began to flash in front of her eyes and the pressure in her head perched on the verge of explosion. Her own panicked pulse was pounding so hard in her ears that she never even heard the crash.

A shower of glass peppered her hair and face, but it was only when Dan ducked, letting go of her throat to shield his eyes that Karly realized she could hear snarling. In the next instant, Puppy was on them both, flecks of glass from the shattered living room window and drops of blood falling from his fur as he attacked. A gun went off; Karly hadn't even realized Dan had pulled it from his jacket holster, but she both heard and felt the whiz of the bullet pass through her hair.

She screamed, but then so did Dan as Puppy's jaws snapped onto his arm. Dan dropped the gun when the wolf shook him, yanking him off balance and off Karly, and letting go only when Dan hit the floor on his knees. That's when Puppy went for his throat.

"No!" Karly screamed, but even as it was happening, she honestly didn't know who she was trying to stop—Puppy, savagely pressing his attack, intent only on getting his strong jaws around Dan's vulnerable neck…or her ex-husband, who was fighting back, kicking, punching, and already reaching for the concealed revolver he kept as a backup, tucked under his shirt at the small of his back.

Karly dove for the gun, lying where it had fallen on the carpet. She saw the glint of light flashing off the shiny nickel-plated revolver when Dan raised his hand, but she got hers up first. They were less than six feet apart. He could have shot her first had he noticed what she was doing, but he didn't notice and Karly had no desire to warn him. She simply shot. Not once or twice, but over and over again

The sound in that tiny rental cabin was deafening. She honestly didn't know if it was the sound alone that sent Puppy leaping to get out of the way or if she'd accidentally shot him. That she didn't accidentally shoot all three of them was nothing short of a miracle, because she didn't stop firing until the bullets were gone and the slider snapped out and locked.

If she hadn't been such a coward, she would have shot Dan. But she was a coward. She'd wasted every bullet in that gun, shooting up the floor between them instead.

Panting, her hands shaking violently and her finger still fighting to pull that trigger, Karly stared into the wide and furious eyes of her ex. He blinked once and then again.

"You fucking crazy bitch," he breathed, incredulously.

She had no bullets left, but Dan did. The gun in his hand was trembling, but he seemed to have forgotten he had it. He only stared at her, his shock visibly building back toward fury just before his gaze slid slightly past her. She didn't realize he was staring just past her shoulder until she saw the anger in him suddenly melt into shock.

"Put that god-damn gun down," Colton growled behind her, "or I'll rip your fucking throat out."

It was the fear on Dan's face that made Karly turn around. She already knew what she was going to see and, oh, but how she didn't want to.

She heard the clatter when Dan dropped his backup gun. She dropped hers too. Not just because it was empty and useless, but because Colton was crouching on all fours between her and the kitchen, where she knew for a fact he had not been bare seconds before. He was bleeding, rivulets of red dripping down the length of his arm from where a bullet she'd fired had grazed him and from all the tiny cuts that coming through that living room window had left on him. Worst of all though, he was naked. Completely unabashedly naked, with Puppy's brand new collar decorating his neck.

His teeth were bared. He was growling, like something savage—a very convincing something savage—and he was...rippling. His muscles kept bunching, flexing; the leap that would bring him right back into the fight barely held in check, while his very flesh buckled in and out with a strange fluidity. He still looked human—of course, he did; how else was he supposed to...look? And yet, he also looked very much like something else. It was in his eyes. Those yellow, yellow eyes that remained locked on Dan, ignoring her completely even when her legs suddenly gave out under her and Karly sat down, right there in the middle of the bullet-riddled floor.

"Puppy," she whispered, wishing more than anything that her eyes were lying to her.

For the first time, Colton dragged his lupine stare from Dan to her. He tipped his head, an animalistic shiver rippling through naked flesh. "Karly," he growled, struggling to get the words out of a still too-wolfish throat. "Sweetheart, please stop calling me that."

CHAPTER ELEVEN

"We can't cover this up," Gabe said as Colton glanced back across the room to where Karly sat swaddled in a patchwork quilt on the couch. Mama Margo was watching over her, trying to feed a little coffee mixed with a lot of moonshine into her.

"It'll help," Mama Margo kept saying, but Karly wasn't responding. She was doing what she'd done pretty much from the moment he had transformed in front of her. She was staring at him. Just staring. Her face was a blank canvas, absolutely void of any discernable expression. That in and of itself was very telling, but not in any way that made Colton happy.

Tied hand to foot and gagged, Dan was in the kitchen, tucked back behind the half wall so Karly wouldn't have to see him. Currently, Marcus was keeping him company. The lanky Omega was hunkered down directly in front of him, forearms braced across his knees, his eyes bright yellow. He didn't move. His teeth all but bared, he didn't speak either, but every few breaths if Dan so much as twitched, Marcus growled. So far, that had kept Dan incredibly still and absolutely silent.

Every bit as silent as Karly was being. Colton looked at her again. He wished she'd say something, do something. But from the moment he'd tied Dan in the kitchen, dug his clothes back out of the bushes where they'd been stashed and called this whole clusterfuck in to Gabe, she'd only spoken once: "Were you in my bed last night?"

Had Colton known that was the opening shot of a completely different battle rather than just a plea for clarification, he'd have chosen a completely different answer. "Do you know I'm real now?"

When she'd said that to him last night, it had stung every bit as badly as the physical cuts he bore now. He had poured his whole being into loving her. He had held her in his arms and in his eyes, and she had held him back, gifting him with the most beautiful surrender any woman could give a man. And she thought she was dreaming? He should have made his reality clear right then.

Who was he kidding? He never should have transformed in her bed in the first place, but the desire to see her with his human eyes, to touch her with his hand instead of his paw, had been just too overpowering.

Not that any of that mattered now. There were now two non-*volka* people in this room who now knew the secret behind Hollow Hills. That Karly was one, Colton didn't mind so much. He wished she'd found out a different way, but he felt sure she'd keep their secret. Dan, however, was a completely different matter.

"Cole." Lowering his voice, Gabe moved to block Karly from his sight and perhaps reclaim Colton's attention. Which left Colton staring at Dan—Marcus was enjoying himself; the big, tough wife-beating cop wasn't making a whole lot of noise right now. Colton couldn't look at him too long before the urge to rip his throat out began to well up all over again. "Cole!" Gabe snapped. Finally succeeding in catching Colton's gaze, he lowered his voice. "We *can't* cover this up."

"I heard you the first time," Colton said. "It couldn't be helped."

"I know that." His expression said he wouldn't mind arguing that point, but Gabe held up surrendering hands, preferring instead to tackle the most pressing issue first. "I know it, I do. And he—" Dan shrank from Gabe's accusing finger as far as his bonds and the kitchen wall would allow. "—he knows it too, but his cop buddies out in Redemption…they don't know, and probably wouldn't even believe it if you got the whole damn thing on video! He's going to go home, spin this story to his best possible advantage, and then they are going to come back here."

"They won't believe him," Colton scoffed, sounding far more certain than he actually felt. "What's he going to say: I see werewolves? They'll laugh him off the force. If he's not very careful, he'll end up with a psych-evaluation and be stripped of his gun. What he ought to be more worried about right now, is my arresting him and how the hell he's going to spin the attempted murder of his wife to his friends back home!"

Dan looked at him now, and for the first time, some of that nervous fear disappeared behind a thin veil of dark calculation.

Marcus growled again, but Dan continued to stare at Colton until Marcus reached out a slow hand to take him by the throat. He leaned into Dan, coming in so close that the two men had to be breathing the same air. Marcus tipped his head, filling up the tied man's entire field of vision. By the way Dan's face began to redden, he was probably squeezing, cutting off his air.

"Don't look at him," Marcus murmured, soft as any lover. "I'm right here. You look at me, *chelovak*."

The urge to give the order to snap Dan's neck was every bit as overwhelming as his desire for Karly had been last night.

Gabe snapped his fingers in Colton's face, twice. "You're going to arrest him?" he said incredulously once Colton's eyes had locked on him again. "Are you insane?"

"I'm not letting him go." Colton let his eyes drift back to Karly. She hadn't moved. She was still staring right at him, her face drawn, still ignoring Mama Margo and her moonshine strength elixir. He wanted to comfort her, but he had a feeling if he went to her now, comfort would be the last thing she took from him. "He's going to pay for what he's done."

He looked at Dan again, swallowing back another surge of savage fury. Why the hell did he have to show up now—show up at all, even—and ruin what fragile progress he and Karly had made? He couldn't remember the last time he'd wanted to hurt a human the way he wanted to hurt this man now. His muscles kept flexing, the wolf in him pressuring its way up through his guts until the pulse to shift was all he could feel pounding at the back of his head. If he looked in a mirror right now, he knew all that he would see would be the wolf, bright in his yellow eyes. It was already heavy in his tone, turning his voice raspy and gruff. "I swear it, he's going to pay."

"He's going to pay?" Gabe stared at him, disbelief abruptly giving way to hard laughter. "What exactly are you suggesting we do?" He lowered his voice now too, the wolf shining yellow in his own eyes as he shifted to block Karly once more out of Colton's sight. "I know it's hard, but think about what you're doing. Give the order and I'll follow it, but the days when we could disappear little problems like this out in the backwoods are long and truly gone. If he goes missing, people will come looking for him. And if he turns up dead…well then, welcome to the twenty-first century: the great age of forensic achievement. No one can find Bigfoot, but in the hunt for a dead cop's killer, I guarantee they're *gonna* find a werewolf!"

He was right, and Colton knew it. But he was just pissed off enough to make thinking through the problem difficult. He kept glancing at Karly and his warring want of her, plus his need to make sure she never had reason to fear a return visit from this sonofabitch, made clear and rational thought impossible.

"We're in the middle of a Hunt," Gabe said, helping to keep him focused on the problem and the fury of the wolf tamped down. "We can't have a bunch of outsiders from two different states poking around, looking for evidence and interfering in the breeding affairs of people who don't care for humans or cops, and especially not for human cops. All it will take is one wrong word to the wrong *volka*, and the next thing you know, someone on our side is going to get irritated, someone on their side is going to grab their gun, and then someone's going to get killed. God help us if a *volka* draws first blood, but God help everyone if a human does! It'll be the Dark Ages all over again with huntings and burnings, entire packs wiped out of existence, and before you can say 'piss in a bucket', we'll be at war! And this time we'll be annihilated, Cole, because unlike before, nobody's going to hold back in the hopes of finding a peaceful solution. Hollow Hills was that solution. If they come after us here..." Gabe shook his head.

Stabbing fingers from both hands through his short, dark hair, Colton tried to think beyond the anger. "I'll talk to people. I'll stress the need for patience—"

"How patient are you feeling right now?" Gabe asked bluntly. "And no offense, buddy, because you've always been Alpha to me, but you haven't taken a mate, you've barely participated in the Hunt, and right now, McQueen is a stronger leader in the eyes of this county than you are. Nobody is going to listen to you, and the last thing McQueen will be when the *chelovak* start invading is patient."

"Drink, damn it," Mama Margo said gruffly, drawing everyone's attention back to where Karly was stubbornly ignoring the drink in favor of shrugging out of her quilt.

"I'm fine," she whispered, but her hands were shaking and so was her voice. Every inch of Colton came into sharp focus when Karly crossed the room, coming to within feet of him. She didn't look at Dan. She just stared at Colton, at his eyes in particular. At his mouth.

He looked at her mouth too, the almost desperate need to kiss her sinking into his gut like claws. He tried to take it as a good sign that at least she didn't seem afraid of him, but she was still wearing that expressionless mask and heaven only knew what her thoughts were like underneath.

"What are you?" she finally asked.

It wasn't screaming or shouting, or crying; Colton hoped that might be a good sign too. "They called us *volka*."

"You're not gypsies," she guessed.

It was a struggle to keep the wolfish gruffness out of his voice. "No."

She hesitated, all but flinching as she said, "A-are you a werewolf?" For the first time, her mask cracked, giving him a glimpse of the confusion writhing within her. "Is…is everyone a…?"

She didn't say the word again, but then, she didn't have to. He knew what she meant.

"Yes." He tried to reach for her, but she withdrew even further, already shaking her head.

"The w-whole town?"

"No," Colton tried to assure, before Gabe added, "We have maybe fifteen, twenty humans in Hollow Hills. Most are half-breeds, though."

"So, I'm not the only…" 'Normal' was right there on the tip of her lips. He watched her stumble over trying not to say it before the one phrase she'd heard here suddenly made sense. "…*chelovak* here?"

"Good save," Gabe muttered.

"No, you're not," Colton said, frowning at him.

Karly glanced to her husband. "What happens now? What are you going to do with him?"

"I'm going to make sure he never hurts you again."

"How?"

Colton knew better than to answer that. He'd sooner dig his own heart out with a spoon, than to make her share any part of what he intended for Dan. It was the hardest thing he'd yet done today, but he made himself turn away from her. "You're not staying here anymore. Go with Gabe—"

Karly shook her head.

"He'll take you someplace safe."

"Where?" she countered. "Your house?"

He looked at her, but did not bother feigning either surprise or offense by her suggestion. His house was, frankly, the safest place in all of Hollow Hills. Both from outsiders and from its less understanding residents. And with her living under his roof, that would give him all the time and ready opportunities that he'd need to bring her back to where they'd been last night. Except the next time, there would be no doubt in her mind as to whether or not he was really there, lying with her, pouring himself into her.

"Go with Gabe," he gruffly repeated.

"No."

He reached for her arm, but Karly flinched, shrugging away from him, her hands held up as if she fully intended to shove or slap at him if he tried to touch her again. Colton frowned, not at all liking it that she was looking everywhere but at him now. Her eyes were strange—wide, angry, confused…hurt. Her gaze kept jumping from one fixed point in the kitchen to another, though none of those points were people, *volka* or otherwise. Dan grunted, his first pleading mew not to be left behind, but that mew was abruptly cut off when Marcus's hand on his throat clamped down hard.

Karly moved then, but it wasn't toward Dan. She retreated back out of the kitchen, crunching broken shards of glass into the carpet with every shallow backwards step that took her closer to the front door.

She tripped every one of Colton's 'rabbit' sensors. She was going to run.

"Karly." He stalked after her, catching her arm to stay her and refusing to let go even when she tried, just once, to shake him off. "Look at me."

She did, but that more confirmed, rather than eased his fears. She was definitely going to run. He could see the decision as bold as the blue of her eyes; she was going to wait until his back was turned, and then she was fleeing.

"Don't be afraid," he tried to say, but it came out sounding like begging. 'I will take care of you, I swear it.' Those words were perched right there at the tip of his tongue, followed by an even more emasculating plea for her to 'Stay.' Just stay. That was all he wanted. His need for her burned inside him like living coals, and they barely even knew one another. 'Don't make me have to hunt you down', would have sounded too aggressive and only served to scare her more. "Please," he whispered instead.

He couldn't remember the last time he'd begged anything from anyone. It had probably been his father, and it had probably been to get him to stop beating his mother. It left a bad taste in his mouth this time too, and Karly still didn't listen. She pulled, gradually increasing the amount of strength it took until Colton had no choice but to hold her arm so tightly he would hurt her or let her go. He chose the latter. He wanted her to stay, but not if he had to do it through force alone.

Karly retreated, but those two small steps may as well have been miles for the all the distance they represented. "You can't keep me here. I haven't done anything wrong, and I don't want to stay."

"Oh, piss on all this puppy love nonsense!" Mama Margo suddenly spat, startling everyone. "There's more at stake here than either of your wants or wishes!" Giving everyone an equally hard glare, she stalked past everyone to dump the moonshine down the kitchen sink. Slamming the glass down on the counter so abruptly that it was a wonder it didn't shatter, she gripped the edge of the sink. Frowning, she glared at the drain for the longest time before her eyes narrowed. "Disappearing him will only delay the inevitable, but a delay is better than having an army of *chelovak* lawmen tromping through our Hunt." Twisting her head, she gave Dan a dispassionate once over before fixing equally hard eyes on Colton. "Get rid of him."

Having only just been allowed to breathe unobstructed, Dan began to struggle, his gag poorly muffling a long string of alternating curses and pleas that escalated into shouts when Marcus grabbed the front of his shirt and hauled him roughly upright. Lanky he might be, but there was real strength there as well. He tossed Dan up over his shoulder as if the tall and burly cop were nothing more than cumbersome baggage.

"Piss on me," he warned as he carried Dan, kicking and flailing, right out the back kitchen door, "and I'll fucking neuter you."

"I don't care how you do it," Mama Margo said, once they were gone. "Just make sure it doesn't come back to nip at our tails before the Hunt is over. And you—" She turned hard eyes on Gabe. "Clean up this mess. Get rid of his car, the guns, any trace you can find that he ever came here, and fix my damn house. There's bullet holes and glass everywhere. As for you—" She turned on Karly last. "—your husband never came here, you've not seen the sonofabitch since you left him, and you've no idea where he's gone. Now, go pack an overnight bag. You're coming home with me."

"No." Karly tried again to refuse, but the thing about Mama Margo that eventually everyone came to know very well, was she never took 'no' for an answer. Not once she'd made up her mind.

"Pack," the old woman said again, her honeyed eyes flashing and brightening. She also was not in the habit of repeating herself.

Looking from Colton to Gabe, and then back to Mama Margo again, Karly gave in. A few minutes later, with all her worldly belongings packed into her single suitcase, she followed Mama Margo out the front door and down the three porch steps. She never even tried to look around the side of the house for one last glimpse at Dan. Colton took comfort from that. Whatever else she might be feeling for her soon-to-be ex-husband, obviously Karly was not nursing a broken heart.

Of course, she didn't look back at him either. Drawing the same conclusion for himself cut Colton all the way to his core.

"Shit," Gabe said, once they'd gone. He scuffed the heel of his boot at the ruined carpet. "I'm going to have to go all the way to Lowe's for flooring."

"And a new window," Colton said distractedly, watching from the open doorway until he couldn't see even the dust cloud kicked up by Karly's retreating car. "And a saw."

Gabe arched non-committal eyebrows. "You want to use it first?"

Turning, Colton went to the back door. Marcus had carried Dan out to the old woodshed, dumping him in the leaves and dirt next to the old chopping block. The little rental cabin didn't even have a wood-burning stove anymore, but the lean-to was still standing there, partially reclaimed by twining ivy and blanketing moss, and even had a good cord of well-seasoned wood stacked inside. Where he'd found the axe, Colton didn't know, but Marcus stood over Dan, idly swinging the old tool, stretching and limbering up while he waited for the command. The axe was more rust than metal now, and dull as hell. This wasn't going to be quick or pretty. It was, in fact, just the sort of death a man like Dan deserved.

"No." Colton looked at Dan, lying flat on his back, his shaking hands pleadingly trying to ward off the first impending blow. He looked sickly, pale, with beads of sweat popping out all across his brow. Deliberately, Colton made himself smile. "No. I think I've got something else in mind for our little, wife-beating friend."

CHAPTER TWELVE

Mama Margo's home was very similar to the log cabin Karly was renting from her. It was small, remote, well-suited for just one person, and decorated nothing like what she would have expected a…well, a werewolf's house to be. How odd was it to even have that preconception? She honestly didn't know what she ought to expect. Dirt floors, maybe, but that's not what she saw peeking in through the open screen door. Dead rabbits or other small animal pelts hanging from the trees and bones from the eaves. Maybe herbs and cauldrons or other witchy-backwoods-mountain woman things lying about. But no, the place was very clean, very tidy, sparsely furnished with only the barest necessities, and the only frivolities that Karly could see were in the two lace doilies that decorated two small tables—the two-person kitchen table just inside the front door, and the end table situated between two chairs on the front porch.

"Sit down," Mama Margo ordered, pointing at the first of the two chairs.

Hugging her suitcase (in which she had packed the most random assortment of belongings, and which did not—as she would come to discover a few hours later while readying herself for bed—include either a night shirt, a toothbrush, or even a matching pair of socks), Karly ignored the first chair and sidled up to the farthest instead. She sat, nervously watching as Margo accepted the other seat. For the longest time, the two women simply sat, staring at one another, the heavy silence between them occasionally interrupted by birdsong, crow caws, and the sporadic plink-plonk-plunk of a pinecone bouncing off the tin roof.

"Damn squirrels," Mama Margo said. "Every now and then I go out and shoot one, crockpot and eat it; it don't matter. Randy little bastards just make more squirrels."

Karly had no idea if she was supposed to commiserate or keep quiet.

Folding her rough, weathered hands together, Mama Margo took a deep breath. "How you feeling?"

Karly had no idea how to answer that either. She supposed she ought to be scared. Maybe that would come later, but right now everything felt too surreal for her to be afraid. "I don't know," she admitted.

"Where do you think you'll run to?"

"I don't know," she said again.

"Where do you think you'll run," Mama Margo repeated, "that he won't eventually find you? Because he will search. He won't be able to stop himself. And I don't mean that little pig shit you married. I mean the other one. The one who wants you despite the fact that you are entirely the wrong female for the job." Turning in her seat, the old woman leaned toward her. "He is an Alpha, girl. He does what he has to—whatever needs doing; regardless of what he would prefer—for the good of the pack."

Karly looked at her.

"Does that frighten you?" the old woman asked.

It ought to. But no, Karly slowly shook her head.

Mama Margo's hard expression didn't so much as twitch. "Why not?"

Because regardless of what else he was, Colton wasn't Dan. He wouldn't hurt her.

"Say it out loud girl," Mama Margo told her. "Know it for the truth it is."

For the first time all night, Karly felt the prickling approach of tears burning in behind her eyes. She dug her fingers into her bag until her knuckles hurt and bit the inside of her cheek, just to keep those tears in check. "I can't do this. I…I just can't."

"Too damn bad, because we're going to do this all damn night if we have to." Slapping her hands against her knees, Mama Margo pushed to her feet. "I'm going to make a pot of tea. So cry yourself out if you have to, but then we're going to talk. There's things you need to know if you're going to stay here. And if you're not, well, there's things you should know then too. Not the least of which is just how badly we'll be fucked without Colton, since we both know, wherever you go, he's going to follow you. You're in his nose now, girl."

"I didn't mean for this to happen."

Mama Margo frowned, showing her exactly what she thought of that sentiment. "What you meant or didn't mean makes little difference now. It's what you do *next* that's going to affect us."

She went inside, leaving Karly alone on the front porch, feeling the whisper soft kiss of the morning breeze washing across her face and listening to another bouncing pinecone. Setting her suitcase on the floor between her knees, she picked at an unravelling string near the worn zipper. All she'd wanted was to escape the trap of a bad marriage and find a safe place to hide. Now if her husband wasn't dead—her chest tightened—then he soon would be, and here she was, quietly accepting it and no less trapped than she had been before.

Except that wasn't quite true, was it? She *was* trapped, but instead of being stuck in a house of violence with a man she had once loved, but now had come to fear and despise, she was now stuck in a town full of *volka*—her brain faltered at calling them werewolves. Hollywood had werewolves; fantasy books had werewolves; paranormal romance shelves in bookstores around the world were absolutely littered with love stories about werewolves; real life did *not* have werewolves!

And yet, here she was.

Combing her hands through her hair, only just resisting the urge to pull, Karly reached back along her shoulder until she felt the tenderness of Colton's love bite. Her chest felt as if it were caught in a vise, and yet a slow pulse of heady arousal came thumping instantly, incredulously, to life between her legs.

She didn't love him; she barely knew him!

But she liked him. He made her feel safe.

He wasn't human. How often did a girl get the chance to say that about the man threatening to court her, whether she wanted him to or not?

Honestly, how could she still feel this tiny thrill of excitement budding up inside her just at the thought of him coming after her, his muscles flexing to take her, his lupine eyes burning with the intensity of his determination and desire?

Even more honestly, how could she leave when she still had no place to go? She didn't want to return to Redemption, back to the house she'd shared with Dan, filled as it was now by nothing but ghosts and ugly memories?

They were going to kill Dan, and all she had done was walk away from it. She wished she could make herself feel something about that too, but maybe she was still too numb. All she wanted to do on that front right now was watch. Maybe even help.

Karly hugged her stomach, feeling just angry enough and just sick enough to recognize that for the lie it was. She didn't want Dan dead, but she still wasn't jumping up to stop it.

Talk about empowering—the way it had felt when she'd held Dan's gun and emptied every last bullet into the floor between them...the way her husband had stared at her, at first shocked and then affronted—that had been so damned cathartic. Karly hugged herself, shuddering because in that moment, all she could feel was the kick of the gun back in her hand. One way or another, he was never going to hurt her again. He was never going to call her, scare her, whisper his ugly things into her ear. Colton was going to see to that.

But none of those was any kind of reason for her to stay in Hollow Hills and...what? Marry Colton, or just mate with him?

Her sex pulsed again, another heady throb of heat and wanting that had absolutely no business being in her body on the same day that she found out the guy she was just starting to seriously like was a real life Wolfman.

Mama Margo came back out onto the porch, bearing two steaming cups. She set one on the table next to Karly. "So," she said. "What excuses have you lined up?"

She honestly didn't know where to start. "Why me, Margo?" Karly countered. "What is this, a wolves mate for life sort of thing?"

The old woman snorted into her tea. "They don't, you know. And neither do we. We form attachments, fall in love, and either live happily ever after or get our hearts broken, just like everyone else. Our divorce rate is probably on par with most *chevolak's*...for everyone except Alphas. It's a rare thing when an Alpha mates with a woman he loves; it's even rarer when he divorces. Sacrifices must be made when it comes to the good of the pack. Everyone knows that. It is the price both Alphas and their Brides pay when they choose to lead."

"I'm not choosing to lead," Karly tried to protest, but Mama Margo slapped that aside with an impatient wave of her weathered hand.

"Neither did I. I was called, same as you are being now. But I did my duty. I accepted my Alpha and I bore him seven strong sons, all of whom met their end before their time. The Deacon himself killed my mate. McQueen's sire repelled that invasion attempt twenty years ago, but he sickened and he died, and now it is Colton who has stepped in to lead. And what does the Deacon Alpha do? He brings his son to our Hunt, and his daughter…in hopes that Colton—or Sebastian McQueen—will take the bait. Ha! I knew his teeth when he took my husband, and I know them now." Mama Margo looked at her, the yellow of her eyes burning hot. "I will have a *chevolak* Bride long before I ever allow a Deacon bitch to set foot on my land."

"I'm sorry," Karly said. Mama Margo never once allowed her pain to show, but it was there all the same, hidden under verbal barbs of bitterness and mask of strength. "I really am, but I am not the girl you're looking for."

Margo physically turned her chair around so she could face Karly fully, pinning her to her seat with narrowed and calculating eyes. "You, girl, are the only human I have ever seen stand firm against one of us. Not once, not twice, but three times you met the Deacon bitch's charge and you did it in the middle of a Hunt on our own damned field. Ha! The insult was priceless."

"What insult?" Karly almost laughed at her, it was so incredulous. "I got my ass handed to me all three times! She knocked me down, Margo. She did it effortlessly!"

"But you kept getting back up. No Alpha has ever to my knowledge taken a *chevolak* Bride. Omegas, yes, cast out to wander among your people, how can they help but take outsiders for mates? Lieutenants, perhaps, upon occasion, if the circumstances are right. But never an Alpha and never in a Hunt. But last night as we watched you stand to meet the Deacon's daughter's repeated attacks, I heard the whispers. She bared her teeth at you, and you…you didn't even flinch. That kind of strength is impressive, girl, and I don't care who or what you are. Neither, apparently, do many of my fellow residents here in Hollow Hills. If Colton takes you for his Bride and I give my consent, his choice will not be met with censure. I'm sure of it. In fact, your display was so impressive, if McQueen takes you to Bride, he may very well steal the position of Alpha on your popularity alone."

Her jaw dropping, Karly shrank from what Margo was saying. She almost laughed all over again, only this time it wasn't funny. "What do you mean, McQueen? Are you saying I'm in your...your Hunt now whether I want to be or not?"

The old woman gave her another calculating stare. "If you leave, McQueen will not follow you. He'll pursue his interest in the Hunt. He'll make his choice, run his Bride to ground and then move to take the Alpha-ship. But Colton...Colton is drawn to you. If you leave, he will abandon us to follow, because you have aroused in him a need I don't think he's felt since childhood." When Karly only stared, waiting, Margo said, "The need to protect."

"I don't need protecting anymore." For the first time, Karly looked away, unable to hold that knowing stare. "You've already taken care of that."

"You're protected so long as you remain with us. Leave, and you'll be as exposed as you ever were."

"But Dan..."

"Will get what he deserves. But there are consequences to what we have done, and you know they will follow your footsteps every bit as doggedly as Colton will." Margo leaned back in her chair, her worn hands resting lightly upon the equally worn wooden armrests. "What do you want, child? Think now. If it were in our power to give it, what would you have? Colton is a good man."

"I don't love him," Karly protested.

Margo scoffed. "You don't know him. You've been here, what, a week? Who falls in love in a week? A fool, that's who, and one who is destined to fall right back out of it again just as quickly. Nobody says you have to love him. Ask yourself instead, do you like him? Do you like the man he is? What he stands for, what he does? Do you respect him? If you can say yes to those things, then the prospect for love is already there waiting to grow between you. If your naughty bits are achin' for the chance to bump and rub against his, then so much the better. Good matches have been formed from less, and worse marriages, as well you already know, have started out with more."

Blinking twice, Karly studied Mama Margo. She and Dan *had* started from more. They'd dated for two years. There were still times when she remembered just how happy she had been the night Dan had got down on one knee, proposing to her in front of all their friends. She'd thought then that he was destined to be her One and Only. But then, she hadn't seen his monstrous side yet.

Colton has a monstrous side too, a little voice whispered inside her. But even before her brain had fully formed the thought, she discounted it. Colton might not be human, but he wasn't a monster. Whether the man or the beast, he wouldn't hurt her. He wanted to protect her.

Don't be afraid.

Karly shivered, that familiar thread of heat unfurling between her legs at the thought of what being taken care of by a man like Colton would entail. She thought about that kiss on the field yesterday, when her toes had curled and her belly had turned as hot as molten lust could make it. She thought of her 'dream' and that funny look that had come across his face when she'd told him how she wished that he'd been real. Well, that look certainly made sense now.

In spite of everything, she caught herself trying to smile when she thought of how he'd sat on McQueen's front seat, stubbornly positioned in between her and his perceived rival, growling the whole way home. Puppy had been nothing but gentle with her. Nothing but tender, right from the very start when she'd hit him with her car and he'd still crawled into her bed to lay beside her, comforting her in the only way he could despite his pain.

She didn't love Colton the man, but Colton the Puppy she had given her heart to right from the very start. And it didn't matter what form he was in, he still made her feel safe. No one else did that for her. So while it might take some time—months, if not years—already Karly could see a point in her future when she might fall head over heels for Colton, and in more ways than just the physical attraction that pulled at her now.

"Hollow Hills isn't a bad place to settle your bones," Mama Margo said, still arguing as if she didn't know she'd already won the fight.

"No," Karly softly agreed. "No, it's not." And she already knew she liked at least two of the residents. A touch of giddiness came alive in the pit of her belly as she thought of Colton again. "All right, Margo. I promise, I'm not going to run."

"Are you sure about that?"

Something about the other woman's tone caught Karly by surprise. Her brow wrinkled. "B-but, isn't that what you wanted?"

Mama Margo waved her hand impatiently, as if she could just as easily slap aside Karly's confusion. "What I meant is, there's a time and a place where running is exactly what a woman should do. An Alpha must have a Bride, and Brides are taken in the Hunt."

That giddiness inside her twisted, becoming knots so tight that it was hard to breathe around them. "You want me to enter your Hunt? Is that even allowed?"

"It has the novelty of never having been tried before," Margo admitted.

"What do I do?"

Margo leaned toward her, her amber eyes unnaturally bright. Now that she knew what she was looking at, it was hard for Karly not to see the wolf in the old woman shining through. "Run, girl. I want you to run."

"Where to?"

"It doesn't matter. He'll catch you soon enough."

Every knotted nerve inside her buzzed as if it were on an electric wire. "Then what?"

The corners of Margo's mouth began to curl. Reaching across the table, she covered Karly's hand with her own and very softly, as if imparting the most prized of all secrets, said, "Sometimes a mommy wolf and a daddy wolf, who love each other very much, get certain urges…"

Yanking her hand out from under Margo's, her face burning in a combination of embarrassment and instant arousal, Karly grabbed the doily off the table, wadded it up and threw it at Margo. She couldn't help it. She laughed. So did Margo.

Covering her burning face with both hands, she rubbed as if that alone could extinguish the fire smoldering in her belly. "That's it," she said, giving up. "I'm crazy. That's all there is to it."

Stark raving and completely crazy. Already she could feel the heat of Colton burning into her body…*daddy wolf*… She shivered all over again.

"Totally crazy," she whispered.

CHAPTER THIRTEEN

By the time the sun began to peek its burning face above the horizon, Karly had already been up for hours, immersed to the eyebrows in culture shock.

"Hold still," Mama Margo told her, and Karly did, but she couldn't for the life of her remember any other point in her life when she had been so damned self-conscious of how she looked—not to mention, how she smelled.

"Clothes aren't important," Margo had told her when Karly had blearily rolled out of bed. "You'll be the only one wearing any, once the Brides are presented. It's best to go without, though. Men want to see what they're running for. Besides, the more you wear, the more likely it is to get caught on something in the woods. Not to mention it'll get in the way once he's got you down on the ground."

Karly had flushed hot all the way from her belly to her eyebrows. "We're going to do it right there wherever we drop?"

"No point waiting to seal the deal."

"My divorce isn't final yet."

"Have you signed your fancy, legal papers yet?" Mama Margo countered.

"Yes."

"Then time'll take care of it. Shuck down."

From that point on, everything Karly did revolved around the upcoming hunt. She had to bathe, twice: once to get clean and then again, immersing herself head to toe in brown, thickly-herbed water that smelled like something dead had been marinating in it for at least three days.

"Smells like a possum's behind, but this recipe's been in the family for centuries and believe you me, it works!"

"Oh my God." Karly held her nose, doing everything she could to keep from gagging while Mama Margo washed that smell all through her hair. "They're going to smell me coming from fifty miles away."

"Exactly." Mama Margo thumped her on the head. "Don't expect me to do it all for you. Come on, girl. Get it all up in your privates."

Age and hard living had given Mama Margo the kind of hands that only seasoned fishermen and lumberjacks displayed with pride. A cranky disposition and ill-concealed urgency made them rougher still as she gathered Karly's long blonde hair, beading, braiding, and twisting it up in a series of loops and ponytails behind her.

"There," she said, eyeing the whole mess with critical pride once she was done. "That'll give him something to grip onto."

"I think I'm going to throw up," Karly groaned. "How long do I have to sit in this god-awful stench?"

"Try and do something nice for a *chevolak*," Mama Margo tsked. "Fine, big baby. Get out if you want to, but don't you dare touch my towels! That smell'll never come out!"

Karly ended up standing on a wad of paper towels in Mama Margo's tiny kitchen, drip drying in full display of three open windows

The body paints came out then, and with Karly doing nothing but watching as the kitchen clock worked its way around to 5 am and the slow gray of pre-dawn began to extinguish the stars, Mama Margo began to cover her in dark blue symbols, squiggles and lines. Starting at Karly's shoulders, she let the paintbrush play down Karly's spine before breaking to dash brilliant dots and swirls across her belly, and hips and eventually ending halfway down her left thigh.

"What does it say?" Karly asked.

"What do you think?" the old woman countered.

"Barefoot, pre-pregnant, get her while she's hot, boys," Karly guessed. When Mama Margo sat back far enough to give her a hard look, after a moment, Karly gave her own head a censuring smack. "I'm sorry. I don't know what I was thinking."

Pushing herself back to her feet, Mama Margo came around to Karly's front. Lifting her chin with the tip of one finger, the old woman dabbed a little paint on her brush and then placed a single dot high on the bridge of Karly's nose. The crowning touch was the thin swooping lines she drew directly above the brow of Karly's left eye all the way to her hair line, then from her hair line to the middle of her cheek, and from there all the way down her jaw to her chin.

"The women of my line have worn these markings, if not from the very first Hunt, then from the second. We have no written record. Mothers remember and paint them upon their daughters when their time comes to run. Should you have a daughter, remember these. From this moment, my blood is your blood. My scent is your scent. My line is yours."

The seriousness with which Margo said that effectively sucked the levity from the small kitchen.

"I'm too old to adopt," Karly said, but it was impossible not to feel touched by the sentiment.

"Don't look a gift wolf in the mouth." Mama Margo washed what little paint remained in her cup down the sink. "Wait a few minutes to let this all dry and then you can dress. Just your nightshift, girl. Pants are a waste of time. You won't wear them long enough to make putting them on worthwhile."

As Karly fanned the drawings on her leg with her hand, helping the paint to dry faster, the first fluttering of doubt moved through her. "He probably won't even chase me, you know. There's plenty of other women here. *Volka* women." Prettier. Younger. Steeped in the traditions Colton seemed to prize so highly…

Less damaged than she was.

When she raised her eyes to the kitchen window, it wasn't the lightening sky, but her own reflection she found herself staring at—her blackened eyes, her split lip. This awful smell and her hair, sticking out in a mass of spiky swirls and tangled braids that made the worst case of bedhead imaginable seem fashion-show-runway worthy. She was a mess.

"He'll chase you," Mama Margo said confidently.

"What if he doesn't?"

"He will."

"But—"

"There's no way that boy will stand by while another male tackles you to ground," Mama Margo finally snapped, exasperated. "Especially not if that other male is McQueen. Stop your fretting."

Instead of waylaying her fears, if anything that brought them all exploding to life inside her. "Another male? How many other males am I going to have to worry about?"

"We had a good female turnout this year," Mama Margo said. "Including you now, eighteen bitches are running. Of course, we had a good male turn out too."

"How good?" Karly couldn't believe she was bothering to ask. She already knew she wasn't going to like the answer.

"Forty, forty-five," Mama Margo said airily. "Could be sixty by now. There's always those last minute stragglers who limp in just before the chase starts. Outcasts mostly, looking to snag an easy Bride so they can start their own territories. Try not to get caught by one of those. That's a hard life."

Karly barely heard her. She was still lost on 'sixty'. Her knees weakened. "I-I don't think I can do this."

"Of course you can. Doing this is the easy part. With so many men, every bitch who's willing will be taken, including you. After your display on the field yesterday, I can all but guarantee you'll have some strong males targeting you right from the start. In fact, all things considered, you're probably going to be taken first." When Karly gaped at her, Mama Margo shrugged. "You're human. Humans run very slowly."

It was hard to be offended with facts that were laid out so bluntly.

"Don't worry." Margo softened her previous statement with a conspirator's wink. "We're going to give them all a show worth remembering. They'll be talking about this for years."

Karly would have groaned, but the attempt was ruined since she couldn't even breathe right. "What if I don't want anybody but Colton? What if someone else grabs me, Margo? I-I can't! I just...I *can't!*"

Coming back to her, Margo settled a rough hand on Karly's shoulder. She squeezed. "Do you trust me?"

"Are you crazy?" Karly shot back. She wanted to laugh, but without steady breath that was also impossible. "I don't know you! I don't know any of you! I don't even know what I'm doing here! What was I thinking?"

Margo squeezed her shoulder that much tighter, a grip that felt both comforting and secure. "Breathe," she said.

Karly tried. She sucked a great gasp into her too-tight chest.

"Close your eyes."

Both hands pressing down hard against her own constricted ribs, Karly obeyed. She squeezed her eyes as tightly closed as they would go and struggled to slow her gasping down.

She was still fighting for that when she felt Margo step in close to her and her low voice murmured near Karly's ear, "Clear your mind, girl. Think of the safest place you've ever been; the safest place you'll ever be."

Karly tried, but the first thing that popped into her head was her first night here in Hollow Hill's, lying with her face buried in Puppy's soft fur while the owl from hell stood sentry right outside her window. The second night hadn't been much better, but Puppy had been there for her then too, letting her grip and pull at him every time the thunder crashed and the storm raged on into the very small hours of the morning. He'd been there for her, making safe every scary moment she'd had since she'd left Dan. Karly tried, but no matter what she thought up, nothing felt as safe for her as it had that first time, cuddled up next to Puppy.

And Puppy was Colton.

Karly took a soft breath and held it.

"That's what you're doing this for," Mama Margo said, as if she knew exactly what was in Karly's mind. Giving her one last pat on the shoulder, Mama Margo handed Karly a nightshirt. "Time to go."

"I'll get my keys," Karly said, resigned and grateful that the interior of her car was leather and not cloth. Hopefully the smell wouldn't absorb into the seat.

Hopefully.

"Don't bother," Mama Margo said, already heading for the door. "Nobody drives to the Hunt. We all walk today. Tradition, girl. Tradition is very important. Hope you enjoy three-mile hikes in the early morning mountain air."

"Not particularly." Her legs were aching already.

"Oh well." Mama Margo smirked. "Sucks to be you then, doesn't it?"

"Oh my God, why do I like you?" Karly laughed, and followed her out the door.

CHAPTER FOURTEEN

The three-mile hike to the top of the ridge was in actuality almost four miles because Margo insisted on coming in up-wind of the camp, letting the early morning breeze announce Karly's presence long before they cleared the curtain of trees and brush that skirted Hollow Hill's traditional Hunting ground. Karly didn't know if it was Mama Margo's secret recipe, her foreign humanity, or the fact that she was practically naked, but every eye and nose attached to a male contestant was turned to her. Considering her female competitors were already assembled and already completely naked (apart from their own body paints), she figured her nakedness was the least likely explanation.

If nothing else, the *volka* believed in equal opportunity embarrassment. It wasn't just the females dressed in only a few squiggles of body paints. The men were every bit as scantily attired, and it wasn't hard to tell who was there to participate and who to cheer on the participants. Mama Margo's estimated 'sixty' seemed more like a hundred, especially when Margo leaned into her and whispered, "Take off your shirt. Let them see what they're getting."

"No." Karly flushed, already sweeping the crowd for any sign of Colton.

"Oh, like you're anything they haven't seen before!" she hissed.

"No!" Karly hissed back.

Mama Margo gave her a withering glare, then stepped aside, gesturing for Karly to head on in and join the rest. Glaring back at her, Karly started to, but the minute she stepped ahead of the old woman, she felt an ominous snag at the back of her nightshirt, followed by a loud rip of sundering cloth.

"Oops," Mama Margo said drily, and put away her pocket knife.

It was either let the torn shirt fall and join the others, as if she did the naked body-painted hippy in the woods thing all the time, or just stand there, foolishly trying to hold the cut back of her shirt together.

"You're an evil old woman," Karly told her, choosing the latter.

"See the way they're looking at you." Mama Margo nodded proudly. "My secret recipe. It works every time."

Something was working anyway, because people definitely were staring. Not all seemed pleased. Many, like the buxom blonde daughter of the Alpha Deacon, were openly annoyed. But it was surprising just how many of those naked—plainly aroused—men were staring hungrily back at her.

"Give 'em a good run," Margo whispered to her, and then shoved, that shove being the overwhelming force necessary to get Karly's stilted legs moving again. She still couldn't see Colton, but it was easy to see where she was supposed to go.

The female *volka* were gathering within a roped off corral, held separate from the men not only by a barrier of multi-colored banners, but by an entire football field of grassy distance. Even from this distance, it was plain the males viewed this as an agitating hardship. They were crowded all along the barrier that kept them from advancing, not a pennant-dotted rope, but a hastily constructed three-rung wooden fence. They were tense and silent, completely oblivious to the physical reactions either they or their neighbors were having to the visual proximity of the women, the vast majority of whom pretended not to notice. Nobody was shifted, but all Karly saw among the females was wolfish posturing—the non-existent tail swishes, the preening and strutting, and the enticing aloofness with which the females beckoned potential suitors to 'come hither'.

When she drew near enough, an elderly *volka* standing guard over the female's corral moved to block her way. She frowned at the torn shirt Karly stubbornly held onto, her gaze sweeping what paint lines she could see on Karly's thigh and face. While it looked like squiggles and nonsense to Karly, the old woman must have read something of note because she eventually stepped back and even raised the rope, allowing Karly to join the other women.

She went in like Moses parting the seas. Although her god-awful stink led the way, she doubted that was the only reason for her shunning. As an outsider, she was way out of her element and she knew it. She tried to find a quiet place away from the others, eventually taking up a quiet post by the rope, tucked up between a tree and a fraying green pennant. With some creative folding of the cut halves of her shirt, she was able to prop herself against the trunk without fear of a stray breeze leaving her anymore exposed than she already was.

"*Chevolak*," someone spat. "She has no business here."

"If you can't run faster than her, you've got no business being here either," another drawled, which pretty much silenced the first.

Karly quietly shredded the fraying edge of the pennant and pretended she hadn't heard either of them. She glanced across the field, because everywhere near her was occupied by someone who didn't like her—and that's when she spotted him. In the thick of all those men, Colton grabbed the highest wooden rung to scale the fence, lifting his face to the breeze as if scenting the air.

Could he smell her all the way over there? Heat flushed her, turning her core molten and sending it flowing down onto her painted thighs. Her nipples peaked, tightening and abrading themselves against her torn shirt. She had the most overwhelming urge to break out of her corral and race over there just to apologize for how bad she smelled.

But she didn't.

She was crazy. She was absolutely crazy.

Pushing back off the tree, Karly let go of both ripped halves of her shirt, letting the cloth simply slide off her shoulders, down her arms. She bared herself. Not to the crowd, that was incidental. She bared herself for Colton, and even from all the way across the field. She knew the instant his eyes finally found her. Every inch of him tensed. Naked as he was, that was a lot of inches to drink in, but she couldn't look away. He was rippling, that strange yet beautiful undulation of flesh that meant the wolf in him was fighting to reach the surface of him every bit as hard as he was fighting to keep it down. He wanted her.

That was when she knew, absolutely knew all the way down into the pit of her quivering, knotted stomach, she was going to run…because he was going to chase her.

"They will fault you for many things, you know," Maya purred as she brushed up against Karly's side, "but they cannot fault your good taste in men."

Karly barely took her gaze from Colton long enough to glance from Maya to the three packwomen who accompanied her. Between the four of them, a rainbow of body paints was represented. Yellow, green, metallic silver. Maya was the only one who sported two colors, swirling dots of pink and white that played over her dips and curves. No two women wore the same design.

Maya turned her head, her smile turning sly as she nodded across the female's corral. "If pissing Joela off was your intent, you've managed it."

It wasn't hard to follow Maya's stare to the Deacon's blonde daughter, huddled amongst her tight circle of friends, all of whom sported bruises and scrapes from the day before. "I wouldn't call it intent," Karly said dryly. "It's more like a bonus."

I knew there was a reason I liked you, *chevolak*." Maya bent to briefly rest her chin upon Karly's shoulder. "Don't be offended, my friend, but your stink is marvelous. May I borrow it?"

Before Karly realized what Maya was truly asking, the *volka* caught her shoulders and hugged her. She rubbed, her full breasts pressing hot against Karly's back as she ground herself against her.

Across the field, three more men jumped up onto the fence, craning to get a better look.

"My thanks," Maya said, panting that soft, breathy laugh of hers when she noticed Karly's stunned face. "Don't worry, we'll keep the Deacon bitch off your back long enough for you to reach the woods."

A roaring shout went up across the field, and Karly turned in time to see Colton punch the man standing on the fence next to him. He succeeded in knocking the other man down, only to be ripped off the fence a half second later by someone else. And just like that, suddenly Karly was watching a barroom brawl. Every male erupted in snaps and snarls. It was the most unholy cacophony—more animal than man—punctuated by punches and body slams.

A shiver—half excitement, half apprehension—prickled up her spine like icy fingers.

"Your Alpha is calling to you," Maya whispered in her ear. "I hope you let him catch you, because that is the Alpha Joela was supposed to win."

"Over my dead body," Karly couldn't help muttering.

"Don't say that too loudly. She might comply."

The brawl among the men wasn't easing. If anything, the intensity was picking up. They were making the most unholy baying sounds now, interspersed amidst the growls. They were all rippling now, a chaotic tide moving in every direction at once. Some had transformed already; others were in the process. Karly couldn't see Colton anymore. She tried to look for Puppy, but there was more than one black wolf in the males' corral.

And the spectators, they were everywhere, loosely grouped in family units, content to watch and point, seemingly focused exclusively on neither the males nor the females, but on both collectively. Karly thought she saw money changing hands. It began to feel like Sunday morning at the races, and she was horse Lucky Number Seven. All she needed was a jockey...although with any luck, Colton would be riding her soon enough.

At once both excited and appalled, Karly rubbed her hands against her thighs, smearing the paints there until she caught herself.

"Get as far as you can," Maya told her, her eyes brightening with that oddly lupine yellowish hue. "You're human. If you're brought down too soon, no one will think any worse of you than they already do."

The excitement was building, and it was all around her now. It felt palpable, and just a little bit frightening.

"Where do I go?" Karly asked, tensing now herself.

"Just run," Maya said, growled rather, her voice deepening into startlingly masculine tones.

Karly looked around to find Maya shifting, transforming right there by her side, her whole body rippling in that oddly fluid way as her face distorted, her limbs lengthened and thinned, her back hunched and her fur sprouted at a rate Karly had never seen outside of time-lapse photography. She dropped to the ground, an absurdly graceful canine yawn and stretch easing her into her fully wolfen form. Hollywood had it so wrong. There was nothing painful in Maya's transformation, at least not that Karly could see. No discomfort, not even the slightest wince in the lupine face that turned to her, muzzle gaping in a toothy grin just before the males broke the fence that surrounded them.

Apparently, that was the gunshot she'd been waiting for. The ropes around the females dropped and everyone scattered. With no idea which direction to run, Karly tried to scatter with the group, but she was attacked. Somewhere in the panic, she had lost track of Joela, but when the furry weight of a shifted *volka* hit her sideways, knocking her sprawling on the ground, Karly thought she knew exactly who was snapping for her throat.

It was shocking how strong the woman in her wolf form was. She would have gotten her teeth into Karly, but for Maya and her three pack mates, who leapt into the middle of the fight, snarling, biting, ripping at the blonde's scruff and flanks, and all Karly could do was scramble to get out from under them all without getting hurt. Someone yelped, and Karly felt the spattering of hot blood spray across her back. But there was simply no time to check who it was, because the males had already caught up with them.

Maya sprang away just as Joela was engulfed, every member of that impromptu pack fighting viciously to be the one to cover and hold her. She went down yelping, struggling violently to break free while they squabbled, snapping, biting, ripping into one another and sometimes, in the brutal excitement, into her. It was the football game all over again, only this time no one was playing. They drew blood, theirs and hers; bones snapped, that ominous cracking sound being what finally broke through Karly's shock and launched her back into the race.

She ran, as fast as she could go, her bare feet slipping in the dew-soaked grass, following the path Maya and her friends had taken into the dense forest that surrounded the ridge. There would be no more help from that quarter. The closest things to friends that she had, they were already gone, but that didn't mean Karly was alone. Someone was coming up fast behind her. Right behind her. She could hear the panting and growling, could all but feel the heat of his breath on her back, and both Maya and Mama Margo were right: humans were dreadfully slow runners.

Karly had barely reached the trees when she was tackled. Just as fast, however, the weight that hit her back was knocked off, but it wasn't two wolves that she found herself pinned beneath. It was Seth McQueen, untransformed, naked and painted like every other participant, who wrestled the young grey that had knocked her down into the brush. Without any trace of either anger or enjoyment, McQueen hooked one strong arm around the snarling grey's neck, his other hand latching onto the grey's right front leg. In one savage yank, he broke it.

The grey yelped, with high-pitched screams that erupted into desperate writhing to break free.

Hugging the wounded *volka*, McQueen looked at her. "Run," he growled, a quick nod of his head being the only encouragement she needed to do just that.

She dashed straight through a thick patch of poison oak before she realized what it was, and even then it hardly ranked on her list of immediate concerns. Hoping *volka* were as adverse to the stuff as humans, Karly kept going, only to have that thin hope dashed a few seconds later when she heard the crash of canine paws pursuing her through the leaves.

At least she wasn't the first one tackled. That was the one thought that crossed her mind before two wolves collided directly behind her in a snarling, savage frenzy. Karly didn't look back; she just kept running, up a sharp bluff dotted with thistles that cut at her legs. She barely felt the pain. All she knew was she could hear a stream on the other side of that bluff, and if she could just get to it, then perhaps she might be able to lose the wolves the way convicts in old prison movies lost bloodhounds.

What Karly didn't realize until she was already falling was that the edge of the bluff was not as well defined at the grass led her to believe. She went down on her side, landing with a splash in the mud and water. She barely avoided whacking her head on a fist-sized rock, but she didn't even have time to gasp her shock at the iciness of the water before the *volka* that had pursued her up the bluff leapt down after her.

He landed directly on top of her, a massive blondish-brown beast, the sheer weight of him was astounding. Nothing in his size had prepared her for just how big and heavy he was, although she remembered well how impossible it had been trying to lift Puppy into the back of her car. This wasn't Puppy, though…Colton, rather. This was someone else entirely.

Lying on her back, Karly stared up at him, seeing nothing but muzzle and teeth. He didn't have them bared, exactly, but it was obvious he was struggling internally, as if unsure he wanted to keep what he'd caught. He pawed at her, nudged her chin with his nose, then her breasts, filling his senses with the smell Mama Margo had coated her in. Head low, he slunk off her, then quickly changed his mind and covered her again.

In the distance, Karly could hear the sounds of other captures taking place, other squabbles erupting between males battling to see who was stronger.

The male on top of her heard it too. He moved nervously, flinching at nearby sounds as if expecting to be challenged at any moment. He began to paw at her again, nudging at her shoulder and side. He stuck his nose right up against her cheek, and still Karly lay frozen exactly as she was. She couldn't run without first rolling over, but she knew if she presented her back to him right now, then she was done.

Shaking, Karly's hand brushed that large rock a half second before a crash of brush on the bluff directly above them caught the wolf's attention. Karly didn't think twice. When her hand brushed that rock again, she grabbed it and struck. She'd been aiming for his head, but he jerked back at the last second and she wound up hitting nothing more vital than his shoulder.

The *volka* turned on her, but he only snapped once before a large black blur leaping over the bluff landed on top of them both. As large as he had seemed at first, the blond *volka* must have been younger. It wasn't until she saw him jumping free of Puppy's attack that she realized how much bigger Colton was in his shifted form.

Karly was knocked almost flat on her back in the water. While the stream wasn't deep enough to dunk her completely, it was a terrifying sensation to have her ears suddenly submerged. She came up fighting and flailing, but Colton had already harried the younger *volka* off her. The blond, in the most anticlimactic show of deference, surrendered his conquest and fled in search of an easier catch.

Rolling over, fighting the current and the slippery mud and stones to get her hands and knees on stable ground, Karly crawled for the nearest bank. Every thrashing step clouded the cold water, but no sooner had she grabbed a fistful of solidly-rooted grass than did she feel Puppy's heavy paw step on her back. His teeth caught her nape, sending shivers of absolute panic and, in the strangest twist of what she could only comprehend as depravity, tiny thrills of exhilaration dancing across her skin. Every point of his teeth could be clearly felt as he held her, simply held her, until she stilled again.

He shifted his position, moving to cover her. His front legs framed her shoulders. They were all that she could see of him, though she felt everything—from the familiar comfort of his soft fur, to the heat of his breath, and finally, the release of his jaws as he, gradually, let go of her neck.

Neither one of them moved. Precious seconds ticked by like hours, with her feet still in the frigid water and her knees sinking into the mud and the grass tickling at her face.

The paws and legs began to change, that fluid ripple of transformation turning his fur to skin and his paws back into hands. Puppy's chest against her back became Colton's, naked and hot. His belly brushed her buttocks. His knees braced in the muddy earth to either side of her thighs.

"Shh, sweetheart," he whispered against her shoulder. "It's all right."

Her pent up breath escaped with such shuddering force that it wracked her entirely. She sucked in a replacing gasp, but already the urge to flee was fast melting out of her.

Colton nuzzled her, his human lips brushing back across her nape, not kissing, simply caressing. "Accept me," he coaxed. "Accept me."

She wouldn't be here if she hadn't already. It was a powerful realization. One that left her shaking all over again.

Brushing her hair back over her shoulder, he kissed just behind her ear. He rocked, letting her feel his intent in the not-so-subtle sexual movements as his hips bumped her ass. His voice deepened, turning husky in that way that meant he might look human, but the wolf was right there inside him. "I need you to accept me, Karly."

She loved it when he said her name like that. Not honey or sweetheart or any other meaningless endearment that most people, just tossed out on a whim; but her name, growled in the utmost intimacy while his teeth gently nipped her skin, right where he'd already bitten her—marked her, claimed her for his own—in the dark hours of the night before. She couldn't stop trembling, but fear was the last thing she felt. No, this was something else. Desire, the most primal sensation unlike anything she'd ever felt. It was excitement too, those low thrills that rippled her with every rumbling breath that exhaled from him, only to vibrate into her.

Her skin tingled everywhere he touched her, and he was touching her everywhere. His cock, swollen and thick, cradled as it was in the crack of her ass, rocked in meaningful approximation of what he desired. And with each thrust, the heavy sack of his balls brushed into the shadowy triangle between her thighs to caress her where she ached most to feel his touch.

Quivering anticipation rocked her, much as he was rocking. Every caress made her body tighten and burn. Higher and hotter, a molten screw being twisted right to the snapping point, but in a way that promised pleasure too beautiful to be shared by two people who knew as little about one another as they did.

"Accept," Colton murmured, nipping at the sensitive lobe of her ear.

"I do." Karly whispered, her body instinctively arching back into the sleek entrapment of his own. She tried to hide her face in her arms so she wouldn't have to face the embarrassment of just how much she wanted this. To be taken by Colton just like this, lying face down on the muddy bank. Doggy-style even. How appropriate.

He growled and bit her nape again, his hard body forcing all the softest parts of hers to mold to him. Her nipples tightened, tingling at the touch of his teeth on her neck. Aching for their chance to take a turn in the burning heat of his mouth.

"I do, what?" He moved to the other side of her neck and bit there now as well. Harder this time. The suckling heat of his mouth fastened on her, feasting, marking her as if she were his territory, because she was his territory, and she loved it.

She squirmed in the unyielding prison of his arms, loving the intensity of his possession and the way he took her hands in each of his, weaving their fingers together in a show of intimacy too overwhelming to hide from. "Please!" she breathed.

"Say it," he growled again. He pumped his hips against her, three times in rapid succession, hard enough to make her bottom bounce and a seductive tightening to jolt straight from her sex up to her womb. Liquid arousal flooded her in response. She heard it, the slick slapping sound of his balls bumping her pussy, and the sharpness when he drew his next breath. He could smell it, the heady musk of her pussy as it wept to be filled by him.

"Please!" she gasped. "I-I do accept you! I do!"

He released her hand, but only long enough to guide himself to the entrance of all that liquid heat. Before that first invading push, he quickly re-captured her, weaving their fingers tightly together all over again. They both groaned at his next thrust, the cradle of his strong thighs forcing hers together and making the fit all the tighter for them both.

"Am I real to you now?" The scalding heat of his mouth caught the lobe of her ear, sucking and nipping until it was all Karly could do not to writhe. He rode her slowly, with long penetrating thrusts that pushed him in as deep as he could go. He filled her as if he'd been made for her, poured and molded to all of her most intimate specifications. And when he withdrew, the devastation of thinking he might leave her entirely made her frantic.

"Yes!" She strained against him, arching her spine and pushing back her hips in an effort to force his return. She needed to feel him deep inside her, she needed to feel that overpowering throb that showed just how well they fit together. He was her Alpha. She was just plain his.

His gripping fingers tightened around hers. He rose over her, his long, slow thrusts beginning to quicken. He growled and her sex spasmed, sparking that electrified shiver that brought the beginning of her end. She came much sooner than she wanted to, every inch of her seizing and shaking all around the unending glide of his cock pumping in and out. He lay a ring of hickeys, nips, and gentle bites, all over her neck and shoulders, his bites increasing in pressure as his thrusts quickened, became harder, more aggressive.

His growl and that fastening lock of his teeth on her shoulder made her come again even before the thrilling shocks of the first orgasm completely died away. She wailed into the grass, the overwhelming sharpness of the pleasure he'd brought her more than she could take without bursting into tears.

That's when she felt him come, felt that last vigorous shove slam into her smaller body as he fought to lose himself as deep inside her willing heat as he could get. The hard expulsion of his breath scorched her back and shoulder as he shuddered, spurt after burning spurt washing the mouth of her womb.

"Shh," he whispered, unweaving their fingers to stroke her head and hair. "It's okay, sweetheart. Shh."

"I'm sorry." She hiccupped, sucking at air in an attempt to control her sobbing. "I don't kn-know why I'm c-crying."

Nuzzling at the nape of her neck, she felt it when Colton grinned. "Because I'm just that good, that's why."

Karly couldn't help it. With tears sliding wet down both cheeks, she laughed and was about to roll over if he would let her, a ready remark already springing to her lips, but an interrupting rustle in the brush on top of that overlook bluff stopped them both.

Jerking his hands out of hers, Colton covered her again, his possession now having nothing to do with arousal and everything to do with ownership. He breathed in. His exhale came rumbling out in a warning growl. "McQueen."

"Puppy," came the drawling reply.

Colton began to ripple, his body one threatening motion away from wolfish transformation. Another soft rustle and then the leaves and grass above them parted and Seth McQueen came into view. Fully human, still naked, he gazed down on them, making absolutely no effort to interfere.

"For the record," he said, smirking as he eyed all the parts of Karly that Colton wasn't covering, "I never wanted to be Alpha. Everybody tromping through your property, bringing you their problems day and night, whining and bitching until you settle their petty-ass disputes." He grunted his derision, then his eyes hardened. "A territory needs an Alpha. You want the job; fine. But you fail just one time…you neglect your responsibilities, you give the Deacon so much as a toehold into our town and I won't give you a second chance. I'll take the position from you, even if I have to wipe your pack out to do it."

Colton returned his glare, saying nothing until McQueen shifted his gaze to Karly again. That's when Colton growled, that animalistic snarl that grew by the second with deadly intent.

McQueen never lost his smirk. "Like I said, I hear you…Puppy." Raising his nose, he tested the air. "Damn, that is a beautiful stink." His crooked grimace came the closest that Karly had yet seen to a real smile then, just before his whole frame shimmered and he shifted. Turning, he dropped to the forest floor on all wolfish fours and disappeared into the thick greenery

Colton did not relax, not for the longest time, not until he was sure the other *volka* had truly gone. "I might have to kill him before this is over," he muttered.

"He saved me for you," Karly said. "When I got caught, he knocked the other wolf off me and told me to keep running. He could have taken me for himself, but he didn't."

Glancing down at Karly, his expression softened with slight apology before he grunted. "Come on. We should get back to the Ridge."

What little of the romantic mood McQueen's interruption hadn't killed, died right there.

"Do we have to?"

Colton bent to nuzzle her shoulder. "You don't want to show off your prime Alpha catch? I really am considered quite the catch, you know."

There was that arrogance again. "Yes, you are." Karly smiled, but it faded almost immediately. "But am I?"

He blinked twice, as if surprised.

"*Chevolak*," she reminded, as if he needed one. "Mama Margo said Alphas aren't supposed to take human mates."

"They never have before," he corrected. "But then, no human has ever participated in the Hunt before. Nor in the games that preceded it. I've got the only *chevolak* to ever compete against a *volka*. Some will grumble, sure. Others will think I've snagged the greatest catch in living memory."

"But I lost," she protested. "In fact, I lost on an epic scale."

"But you kept getting back up. Sweetheart, that was pretty damn epic too. That was unheard of. Do you have any idea how many of my people I had to hamstring just to get to you?"

"I was the slowest runner and the easiest catch."

"True. But you were a catch worth fighting for." Colton's smile was as infectious as it seemed genuine. When she smiled back, he chucked her under the chin, took her hand and helped her up off the ground.

They held hands all the way to the Ridge, breaking contact only for those few minutes when Colton helped to wash the mud off in the stream and then boost her up the steep face of the bluff. The Hunt wasn't yet over, but on the way they passed several newly-mated and a few still-mating couples. They passed Joela too, not far from the female's corral, still aggressively fighting to knock her would-be suitors back. Still in wolfish form, the Deacon's daughter kept her tail tightly tucked and her teeth bared. The younger males who had caught her were no longer pressing their suit. A few still whined, trying to wheedle their way closer, but she was having none of it.

"You said there were other Alphas here," Karly whispered as they circled around, giving the squabbling wolves a wide berth. "I'm surprised none of them tried for her. Her family is strong, right? Isn't that part of the politics, strengthening your pack ties by taking mates from other well-established packs?"

"She was caught on the field," Colton said, and by his tone alone Karly could tell that wasn't a good thing. "And she refused all of those who caught her. That's her right, but when you enter the Hunt, the understanding is you do so with the intent to mate. She broke tradition. Like I said, refusal is always the female's choice, but she'd have done better to submit. A stronger male might have thought her worth fighting for if she had."

Joela was eyeing them, the yellow of her eyes baleful and vindictive. She growled only once, so perhaps it was her body posture that gave away her intent. Although they had been careful to keep a proper distance between the *she-volka* and her suitors, suddenly Colton stiffened. He thrust her behind him a bare second before Joela lunged, but the attack was aborted almost before it had begun.

"Do not," a gruff voice behind Karly suddenly barked, "add to our disgrace!"

Jumping, Karly turned to find a much older man, in his fifties, if not his sixties, stalking toward them. His hair was more salt than pepper, but his physique was that of a man accustomed to hard physical labor. The Deaton patriarch ignored Karly and Colton. He went straight to stand between them and his now cowering daughter. Trailing in his wake, cradling the broken arm McQueen had given him to his slender chest, was a man barely out of his teenaged years. He didn't look any happier than Joela, who whined, flashing her throat to her father before crawling on her belly to his feet.

Although the Deaton Alpha did not strike her, there was something about the way he looked at her that reminded Karly of Dan. Nervous, Karly pulled at Colton's arm, wanting to leave, but stopped when his hand tightened on her arm.

The Deaton Alpha turned and looked at them: Colton took the brunt of his glare, but when it eventually shifted to Karly, she saw nothing but disgust. "We're leaving."

Snapping around, he walked away, his children falling into an obedient line behind him. Joela did not transform. She kept her head down and her tail tucked, and she did not look back.

In that instant, Karly pitied her.

Movement from the forest caught her eye. On the far side of the field, McQueen walked out from the trees with a flushed and blushing Maya holding his hand. She flashed Karly a grin, one that faltered slightly when her gaze drifted just beyond Karly's shoulder. Afraid the Deatons were returning, Karly turned, but it was only Marcus and Gabe, both naked and battered. The bright shocks of Gabe's body paints were smeared with dirt and drying blood. He was hugging his ribs. He was also without a Bride and on his face, Karly could see a hurt that ran deeper than his physical wounds when he looked back at Maya.

Maya looked at him for a long time before turning to McQueen. She tried to smile. She also hugged her chosen mate's arm to her naked chest as if he were the greatest treasure and not quite possibly the scariest human being—or *volka* for that matter—that Karly had ever met in her life.

McQueen looked down at her, bemused, then his eyes met Gabe's, Colton's, and finally Karly's. He tipped his head, but he didn't approach. He took his Bride home, giving the Alpha of Hollow Hills an entire field's width of berth.

The Alpha of Hollow Hills.

Her Alpha now too. Karly stepped in to him, hugging his arm the way Maya had McQueen's. Colton gave her the same indulgent smile McQueen had given his Bride. He wrapped his arm around her shoulders.

"Come on," he said. "Let's go home."

CHAPTER FIFTEEN

Karly had packed and unpacked her few meager belongings half a dozen times before she finally just made up her mind. She boxed it up, keeping only those items that had real sentimental value to her, everything that had come from her mother—that silly coffee can for one—just those things that she wanted to keep. Everything else, everything she'd received during her disastrous marriage to Dan, she was in the process of loading into the back of her car. It was all destined either for the nearest Goodwill or the dump (whichever was closest), but she was still sorting and loading it when her phone rang.

Recognizing the number, Karly answered it. "Hello?"

Beth Calloway, her lawyer, did not return the greeting. All business, she started in somberly with, "I have a police officer standing here, a co-worker of Dan's. He wants to talk to you. Now, he doesn't have a warrant, so as far as I'm concerned this isn't official police business. If you say you don't want to talk to him, I'll hang up and he can go fuck himself. It's up to you, honey. What do you want me to do?"

Just the mention of her ex-husband's name dropped an icy snake to writhe in the pit of her stomach. "I'll talk to him," she heard herself say, but her voice sounded weird, even to her.

If Beth noticed, she still handed the phone over, saying only, "Keep it brief. And if you make even the most veiled of threats towards my client, know right now, buster, this conversation is being recorded. I will have your badge."

On any other day, that would have made Karly smile. Beth was a good lawyer. Under better circumstances, they might have been friends. But then the snake in her gut tightened its constrictor grip as she heard the slight shuffle of grips exchanging on the office phone.

It had been almost two weeks since the Hunt, but this had been the one phone call that she'd always known eventually would come: the one where someone from Redemption called to tell her they'd found her husband's body and did she know anything about it. It was the phone call that could potentially put her and Colton both in jail.

Over her shoulder, Karly heard the heavy tromp of Colton's work boots as he crossed the kitchen to refill his coffee cup. "Who's on the phone?" he called through the open doorway.

Karly didn't answer. She turned her back, plugging her other ear so she could pretend she hadn't heard him. Her Alpha carried enough on his shoulders; regardless of what had happened after Margo had swept her out of that tiny rental cabin, regardless of what he'd done to Dan, she didn't want him to worry about this. If it meant keeping Colton safe, she would lie through her teeth for as long as she could. He kept her safe. To return that favor was the least she could do.

"Hello, Mrs. Whitaker," said a man from the other end of the cellular connection. "I don't know if you remember me. I'm Detective Briggs. How are you today?"

Although he spoke light and cheerfully, something in his tone told Karly this man was anything but as congenial as he sounded.

"Barker," Karly corrected. "Dan and I are divorcing and I'll be taking my maiden name just as soon as it goes through."

"Barker, then." Briggs didn't bother pretending he didn't already know that. He kept his mask of cheerfulness too, but he also cut straight through to the meat of the issue with all the surgical precision of a really clever cop. "I have a few questions I need to ask about your current situation, but I don't feel comfortable doing it over the phone. Is it possible for you to—"

"I feel comfortable doing it over the phone and with my lawyer present," Karly softly interrupted. Behind her, she heard Colton come out of the kitchen. She knew he had to be listening. If she'd learned nothing else in these last few weeks, it was that he had phenomenal hearing. It wasn't just her answers he was listening to. He could probably hear Detective Briggs's questions too. "Ask what you have to."

"Fine. I can do that." There was a distinct cooling in the Detective's feigned cheerfulness. "When was the last time you saw your husband?"

"When he beat the shit out of me the night I left him," Karly lied. She did it quietly, flatly, without a shred of animosity to color her words or make of herself a bigger suspect than she already was.

Briggs was quiet. "I didn't know about that."

"You knew he put me in the hospital last year," she countered. "I remember the flowers you and the rest of his buddies sent me. They were very pretty. They came with a card that said you were all thinking of me. Do remember what you said to me when I called you from the hospital, Detective Briggs, and I told you that Dan had put me there?"

"Give me the phone," Colton said, putting his cup down on the coffee table and holding out his hand.

Karly turned her back a second time, holding the phone to her ear with both hands now, just in case he tried to take it. "Do you remember, Detective Briggs?"

"Give me the phone, sweetheart," Colton said, reaching around her now to take it away.

She growled at him. Two weeks living openly among the *volka* hadn't given her much of a vocabulary. She had no clue what she was saying, but she hoped it conveyed irritation.

Colton snorted, then chuckled. "You're so damn cute when you do that."

ABandoning his pursuit of the phone, Colton wrapped his arm around her waist instead. He nuzzled the back of her neck, giving her a gentle nip that let her feel all the points of his teeth. With Dan, Karly had gotten used to wearing shirts that covered her markings; she was still doing that now with Colton, but for entirely different reasons. Instead of hiding bruises from beatings, she was hiding the massive ring of hickey and love bites he liked to mark her with. With Dan, Karly had had to hide to keep people from seeing; but Colton liked for people to see his markings. The more Karly tried to cover them up, the more creative he got about putting them in places impossible to hide. The kicker had been the one he'd put on the very tip of her chin. She currently had enough foundation powders and lotions to open her own boutique.

"I'm very sorry about what happened, Miss—"

Again Karly interrupted, softly, flatly. "You asked me what I'd done to antagonize him. You said he was under stress and that I shouldn't pick fights with a man who loved me as much as Dan did, and who was only trying to provide for me the way good husbands should. Do you remember telling me that, Detective Briggs?"

"That's my girl," Colton rumbled, nuzzling the curve of her shoulder. "Go for the throat."

Briggs was quiet all over again. "Dan says he saw you two weeks ago. He says things got heated, that threats were made. Miss Barker, did you see your husband two weeks ago?"

"No, I did not." Karly didn't even flinch at the lie. Her voice didn't quaver, but every nerve in her body was now standing on end. "Is he there with you now?"

"No, he's still in the hospital. Benton County Psychiatric."

Each and every one of those standing nerves shivered at the same time. "What is he doing in a psych hospital?"

Behind her, Colton chuckled against her neck.

"He was picked up last week by County. They found him wandering naked in a field. He was pretty scratched up, dehydrated, and rambling about…" Briggs cleared his throat. "…werewolves."

Karly could hear the embarrassment the Detective felt at having to say that word on behalf of a man he'd once considered his friend. "Werewolves?" she echoed, letting feigned disbelief drip off every syllable.

"He had some bite marks on him. We're pretty sure he was attacked by animals. It shook him up pretty good."

Shook up, but still alive. She squeezed the phone hard to keep her hands from shaking. "He's lucky they didn't kill him."

"They who?"

Two could play at that game. "The animals."

"You don't sound upset."

"I'm not. I'm glad he's not dead, but to be honest, he's an ill-tempered, wife-beating son of a bitch. And you're the man who let him get away with it for four years, so unless you're accusing me of something…" She let that sentence hang for several long seconds, giving the Detective a chance to either confirm or deny his intentions. He said nothing. "Then, I'm going to hang up."

His tone sharpened. "I still have questions for you."

"I live in another state and I am out of your jurisdiction. Accuse me of something and go through the channels, but I warn you now, it's commendable that you're willing to stick your neck out for your friend, but drummed up assault charges based on the testimony of a man who also says he saw werewolves, isn't going to hold up long enough to go to court. Supporting it just to harass me may even hurt your career. And no, that won't hurt my feelings either. You're a piece of shit cop who's every bit as responsible as Dan for the hell I went through. If you have any other questions, you're going to have to arrest me, because I'm all done talking to you."

Karly hit the disconnect button before Briggs could say anything more. Then she stood there, staring at the far wall without really seeing it. Her hands were shaking. She hadn't realized just how badly until she looked at them. Around her waist, Colton's arm tightened, holding her to his chest because her legs were shaking now too.

"Right for the throat," he said again, grinning down at her.

"Damn," she whispered. "That felt good."

"One down; the rest of his Department to go."

She twisted her head back far enough to see his smile. "You didn't kill him?"

"I can't say I wasn't tempted. But as I told you, we're not monsters. We chased the scrawny little weasel through the woods for most of the night, scared the piss out of him—literally—and then let him go just across the county line. Psychiatric hospital, huh?"

"Yeah." Karly gazed up at him. It might mean she was an awful human being, but she didn't feel even the slightest twinge of guilt. He belonged in jail, but in a pinch, she'd take a mental hospital.

"I guess we followed Mama Margo's edict to the letter then. He won't be coming back any time soon. He might not ever come back."

"But he told people, his co-workers…Colton, Detective Briggs knows—"

"Detective Briggs," he interrupted smoothly, wrapping his arms a little tighter around her, "thinks his buddy is 'shook up' enough to warrant being incarcerated in a mental ward. No one is going to come looking for us. And if they do—" He nuzzled her shoulder. "—all they'll find is a sleepy little town, known for its great hunting and fishing, and filled to the good ol' country brim with very normal-seeming folk."

"And you didn't kill him," Karly repeated. She didn't know why that should make her want to melt a little, but it did.

"Does that weaken me in your eyes?" He tipped his head so he could see her face better, his amber gaze searching hers.

"My Alpha isn't weak," she instantly replied, doing her best to mimic a growl of affront. Oh yeah, she was definitely picking up the lingo.

Colton chuckled. "Damn, that's cute." Loosening his arms, he let her turn far enough for her to put her arms around his shoulders. "Do that again, sweetheart." He backed her towards the couch, his hands already smoothing down over her hips to cup and squeeze her buttocks. "Growl for your Alpha."

"My Alpha," she repeated. It took real skill (and probably a *volka* throat) to form words and growls at the same time, but she offered her best attempt to date. Her knees bumped up against the cushions just as he lifted her, dropping her down to lie across the sofa beneath him.

"Whose Bride are you?" he growled, the amber of his eyes a bold and hungry lupine gold as he made himself comfortable on top of her.

"I'm your Bride." She gasped, her whole body coming to life as his hips moved purposefully over hers, the rub of what was growing into a very promising erection grinding against her pubis. The barrier of both their clothes was a temporary obstacle and one that didn't survive that first hard yank as he ripped her shirt right off her chest.

She'd lost a lot of shirts this way, yet she couldn't quite bring herself to care. Not with the burning heat of his mouth fastening hard upon the peak of her swelling, aching nipple.

"Say it again," he commanded, already feasting to create yet another mark. He plucked and rolled at her nipple's twin until Karly was arching and writhing to the symphony of sensations his mouth and fingers so effortlessly strummed from her.

"I'm yours, I'm yours!"

He tore her pants getting them off her—she lost a lot of pants this way, too—and on the seductive upwards crawl as he rose to cover her again, he paused to press a burning kiss to the smooth skin just above her sex. She saw his nostrils flare and his eyes dilate as he breathed her musk in.

"And I'm your wolf," he rumbled, skinning his pants down just far enough for the denim to be out of his way. His hips burned into her with furnace-like heat. He rocked against her, letting her feel the proof of his desire. "I am yours."

She wrapped both her arms and legs around him as he pierced her, sliding into her slow, hot and deep.

"Yours," he groaned, the mantra by which he took her now. Another nipping bite sparked that mindlessly electrifying moment when her whole world exploded in pleasure so intense that she felt ripped by it.

She was his Bride; he was her Alpha.

He was Karly's wolf.

The End

Printed in Poland
by Amazon Fulfillment
Poland Sp. z o.o., Wrocław